Bumble Bees & White Balloons

A Novel about Navigating <u>Grief</u> and <u>Growth</u>

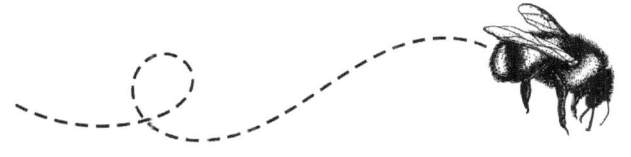

By Safrianna Lughna

ISBN: 979-8-9887681-3-5 (paperback)

Library of Congress Control Number: 2023923395

Bumble Bees & White Balloons
A Novel About Navigating Grief and Growth
Safrianna Lughna

Literature & Fiction > Women's Fiction > Contemporary
Romance > LGBTQ+ Romance > Lesbian > Multicultural & Interracial

Contents

AUTHOR'S NOTE

This story is set in Hampden, MD. The street names and holiday events mentioned are real. The author received permission prior to writing from the store owners of Foraged Eatery (more commonly known as *foraged.* a hyper-seasonal eatery) and Atomic Books to use their businesses as features in some of the scenes. You should check them out because they're rad. The French imPress is not a real coffee shop, but it totally should be.

This slice-of-life queer novel is based very loosely on a real experience in the author's life. The characters are all works of fiction.

SPOILER / CONTENT WARNING

Do not read past this if you do not want spoilers of book content, though no details are given. However, this book contains potentially triggering material!

Some readers may find content in this novel highly personal and difficult. This novel deals with sensitive content including: the COVID-19 pandemic, racism, misgendering, misogyny, miscarriage, body image issues, and disordered eating.

DEDICATIONS

I dedicate my first novel:

To Remy and our angel baby Shaina Elette. This is a tribute to our journey together.

To my wife, Ikenna, who cried so much during the drafting of this book (and will probably cry again when reading it again). You inspire me always and everyday.

To Leora who has always known me as a writer and encouraged me to step into the fullness of myself every moment of our journey together.

To Ariel who has always challenged me to be bigger and better every step of the way with thoughtful feedback.

To Justin for his constant, unwavering support of me in all

I am and do, including my writing. Thank you for being my very first alpha and beta reader.

To Ari and Edlin, my sensitivity readers for Jordan. Thank you for your perspective as BIPOC women and your encouragement in my creative process. I am passionate about inclusion and the ability to see oneself in characters, but I cannot speak personally to all the experiences that deserve to be shared. Thank you.

To every other person on this planet who has lost a child, a dream, or walked alongside themselves through change that seemed impossible to survive. I see you. I love you.

I want to give special acknowledgement:

To Jess Verrill of House of Indigo who has been more influential in my life than she may ever realize. Jess has been an absolute inspiration in the publishing world and helped me move through so many of my visibility issues, energy blocks, and writing questions. Thank you for being my Soul Publisher!

To Justin for really going all in on learning the editing and formatting programs needed to make this book what it is. Seriously, he did the work of a whole team of people! Without Justin's support and dedication to seeing this through, I would have backed down from publishing this for at least another year.

To my many coaches and therapists who have helped me process through my shadow enough to SHINE. Kaela, Lisa, Meryl, Camille, Supriya, Jackie, Jessica, Alicia, Ciscandra, Claudia-Sam, Lily, Lidia, Tamara, and all the other healers who have supported me in my journey–thank you!

To the Itty-Bitty Literary Committee hosted by Jessica Jaxx (J.E. Jackson) for their support and encouragement in the writing process and beyond. What an incredible group of writers and people! Words make a difference.

To myself for showing up to do the work. Way to go, you! You've wanted to have your very own published book in your hands since 2nd grade, and that moment has arrived. Congratulations, and I can't wait to see what you're going to write next.

LIFE

CONTEMPLATION

An act of considering something with great attention; see also: a state of mystical awareness.

JORDAN

It wasn't stars that twinkled, casting a halo behind Abbi's head. It was Christmas lights—thousands of brightly dancing Christmas lights.

Hampden's Miracle on 34th Street was rumored to be one of the most incredible residential Christmas displays in America. Rumored no more. Now that they were there, it was living up to its reputation and beyond. There were thousands of festive decorations casting their colors, blinking, twinkling, glittering. It was basically Abbi in event form. Cheerful. Beautiful. Luminous. Loud.

Jordan felt toasty despite the cold air around them, and it was all because of their wife's enthusiastic grin. She was standing atop a segment of brick barrier pointing at something in the distance. It was in these sorts of moments

Jordan knew no matter what happened, Abbi and them would be two little old queers one day, holding hands and drinking hot cocoa around the fireplace. They got a little wistful thinking about it. But, that was why they'd written the invitation in the "Lesbian Book" last night for Abbi to find in the morning.

Whenever there was a new message, Abigail or Jordan would leave the worn pleather volume sitting on the windowsill in the kitchen right near the coffee maker. It was the perfect place for non-verbal communication, they'd agreed.

December 15th, 2019

You're the kind of girl who cares an unfathomable (see, I can write that word even if I can't say it) amount about decoration. I admire that about you. So for date night... I can't wait to see the Miracle of 34th Street decorations with you! Find your favorite oversized sweater, or two... it's supposed to be a bit chilly. I'll pack a backpack with snacks, and we can walk the Avenue until it's late and maybe swing by Atomic Books or grab dinner from Foraged. I'll get you an early Christmas gift, kay? Come kiss me when you see this. — Jory

Abigail had listened to the instructive, bounding into the

bedroom to wake Jordan with an enthusiastic morning kiss. And now, Abbi was reaching down for Jordan, making a grabby hand with her mitten. Laughing, Jordan pulled themself onto the bricks, tugging Abbi in for yet another smooch. Their breath swelled between them, a foggy white as the chill took it away.

"This is the best date ever," Abbi murmured against Jordan's lips. "I'm so glad you convinced me to move here."

It was their first year in Hampden, a subsect of Baltimore characterized by a diverse crowd, a variety of kitchy shops, and several great restaurants. For Jordan, the best part of all was their ability to take a bus to work, arriving in only a few minutes. Well, that wasn't true. The best part was the way Abbi lit up like a field of fireflies at all the street festivals. The second was the ability to walk less than five minutes to buy a new paperback from Atomic Books any time they liked.

From on top of the brick wall, Jordan could better make out the distant sights. Towering above Abbi by a good eight inches, Jordan liked to tease their wife for all the things she missed.

"Oh... I think I see Santa taking off. Too bad you're too short to see," they said.

Abbi smacked Jordan's arm playfully. "You do not!"

"You're right. But, I'm about to take off!"

Jordan leaped down to the street, took one look back at Abbi, and bolted. Without another look back, they ran down the street towards the heart of the lights and the sound of someone belting out Christmas ballads like never heard before. The owner of the soprano voice had some serious pipes.

But, not as serious as Abbi. Abigail made a wailing sort of sound behind them which cut through the air, then pursued, screeching with laughter.

"Why do you do this to me! You athletic bitch!" she yelled.

Jordan, cackling, slowed their jog and waited for Abbi to catch up.

"You're incredible at being loud, you know," Jordan said.

"Mhm. You like me that way... In bed."

They rolled their eyes, but couldn't disagree.

All smiles, the two linked arms as they began their stroll down 34th Street, surrounded by hundreds of other people. Friends, families, adults, and children. Not only was the crowd impressive, but the party was on. A figure dressed in a Grinch costume was the one singing, and someone was handing out cookies.

It was truly breathtaking—giant inflatable snowmen and snow globes, train sets whirring to life, blinding angels, a tree made of hubcaps, every window, door, and roof lined with light upon light upon light. It was almost hard to look at, but that was alright. Jordan would much rather watch Abbi's reactions anyway.

Beaming and rosy-cheeked, their wife was even more joyous than the decor. Abbi looked like she might faint from all the excitement. Her body vibrated with enthusiasm. Her pale skin glowed with the colors of the street. Jordan loved the way ambient light always seemed to bring out the jewel tones in Abbi's face, sometimes casting peach, others nearly blue. Of course, Jordan had been taken by Abigail's features from the moment they met, enamored with the way her eyelashes were a smidge too long to appear natural, the way her thick brows perfectly framed her round face, and the way her abundance of soft curves could hardly hide in any outfit, including the oversized sweaters she liked to wear so much.

It was hard to believe they'd been together for over two years now and married for one. Their first date hadn't been a date at all, but rather a three-hour conversation in the teacher's lounge at the high school where Abbi taught. Jordan had presented in a school-wide career workshop, teaching the kids about their job in social work and the variety of things one could do with such a degree. When Abigail had walked into her classroom and spotted Jordan, she actually bit her lip. But, as soon as she'd realized what she was doing, and the fact Jordan was staring right at her, she'd stopped, blushed furiously crimson, and bolted to her desk to pretend to organize files.

They'd been inseparable since.

Abbi released Jordan's hand suddenly to take off running again.

"Hey! I thought I was the athletic bitch," they called after her, reorienting to the present to see what Abbi was up to.

She had stopped in front of one of the houses with a window display. From a distance, it was eye-catching with a unique gold and black color scheme.

Wandering over, Jordan leaned in to see what Abbi was seeing.

"Oooh, Jory," Abbi breathed. "Look at the bumble bee."

"You normally don't like bugs," Jordan said, but stooped down anyway to see what she was talking about.

The tree inside was artificial, colored perfectly black. Golden garlands and yellow bulbs spiraled around the branches, and on top, rather than a traditional star or angel, was a crown in hues to match the rest of the decor. There were crystal teardrop ornaments with metallic sheens, a few smaller crowns, and then on the front, an adorable hand-painted bumble bee ornament.

"It's..." Jordan began.

"Bee-utiful," they said together.

Giggling, they swooped in for a kiss, colliding clumsily which only served to produce more laughter. After exchanging a brisk smooch, Abbi leaned in again to look at the delicate ornament.

Abbi covered her mouth suddenly, looking up at Jordan with wet eyes. "It's... So cute." Her voice broke, unconventionally quiet.

"Why are you crying over this bumble bee?" Jordan asked, surprised by the sudden emotion radiating from their wife.

"I don't know. There's something beautiful about this display. Personal, you know? I wonder what the story is."

Jordan's brow furrowed, studying Abigail's reaction. "Yeah... Hey, you okay Babbi?"

There was a moment of silence between them. The street entertainments carried on, crowded with people walking and cars rumbling in the distance, trying to find a place to park and enjoy the evening. Lights reflected off the dampness on Abbi's cheeks, making her a holiday display all the more.

"I've been thinking..." Abbi began, then stopped.

"Thinking about?"

Jordan watched every micromovement of Abbi's face, the flickers of uncertainty, fear, hope—each transformation so easy to read. Jordan knew Abbi like the back of their own hand. No. Better than that. No cliché could encompass it. No stereotype, either.

"What is it, sweetheart?" Jordan reached up to cup Abbi's cheek, turning her toward them. Their deep bronze fingers made a stark contrast against Abbi's now ashen face. Jordan smoothed the palm of their fingerless gloves against Abbi's skin, attempting to create some warmth.

"I know this is probably crazy, but... I've been thinking about having a baby. You know, Mom said the best Christmas present ever would be a grandchild and I guess I've been really taking that in. Having a baby with you would be exciting. I can't imagine anyone else I'd rather raise a child with, you know?"

"I'm, uh, sorta lacking in the parts to do that for you, Abs," Jordan replied.

She winced, visibly stung when Jordan mentioned not having the parts to impregnate her. Abbi looked so vulnerable, an unusual apprehension contorting her features. Her eyes, lit by the nearby decorations, betrayed the intensity of her emotions as plainly as words ever could.

Hesitating, Abbi finally said, "I know, obviously. I... I talked to Josh. He said he would be willing to be a donor."

At the mention of Josh, Jordan felt the hairs on the back of their neck raise. This was surprising coming from Abigail. Honestly, more than surprising.

"When did you talk to Josh about this?" Their bristling wasn't about Josh, at all. Their asexual, aromantic best friend was anything but a threat to their relationship or stability, but the fact that Abbi had been thinking about this recently without any indicator at all was where the shock really settled in.

"Back around Thanksgiving. When Mom mentioned really wanting a grandchild," Abbi said.

Mom again. There it was. Jordan felt the sting before they registered the thought.

That woman was nails on a chalkboard level grating. She had a way of twisting Abigail's heartstrings into a bundle of knots only Jordan could be left to untangle. Regularly. Every phone call, every visit, Abigail was left in a panic, trying to figure out how to impress her mother. The pressure on Abigail was unbearable alone, and the fact that Jordan in no way fit Margie's vision for her daughter was just about too much to tolerate. But tolerate they did for Abigail. Abigail alone.

They could understand her perspective to a degree. Margie had helped Abbi go to college. She'd encouraged Abbi to pursue a future she wanted in spite of all her "radical" choices. She had also helped fund the wedding and showed up like a rockstar mother on the actual day, ensuring everything Abbi needed to be the bride of her dreams was possible.

So, she'd been thinking about this for nearly a month and not brought it up. Jordan could feel their own concerns clawing at the back of their skull. But, they didn't want to make this about them. The last thing Jordan wanted was to seem unsupportive. Abbi had so little support in her life before Jordan, it nearly shattered them to even think of resisting one of her ideas. As a result, though, sometimes all Jordan could do was accept Abbi's flow and go along with the current. She was a force. A tempest sometimes. But they weren't going to be the one to quell that storm.

"So, you've really been thinking about this, huh?" Jordan said. They looped their other arm around Abbi and began stroking her back. "How serious are you?"

"Serious enough that if you gave me the thumbs up, I have a turkey baster and a specimen cup for Josh back at the house already waiting?"

Jordan pulled back, walking a few paces away. Their fingers found the hem of their thick "Dad" sweater and began kneading the neckline for comfort. "Okay. Okay." Their mind was an absolute swirl—images flashing rapidly from Abbi pregnant, to the two of them with a small child decorating a Christmas tree in their house. Jordan knew they would make excellent (if such a thing existed) parents: Jordan worked with kids at the Child Life Center at Johns Hopkins and Abbi worked with teens in high school. They had a nice townhouse, were financially stable, and well, without kids, they had just about everything a couple could want.

One of the joys of being two queer people with uteruses? No surprise pregnancies. But, even though they hadn't taken the steps to make it happen yet, this whole ordeal somehow felt like finding out your spouse was pregnant unexpectedly. At least the baby would look somewhat like them, Jordan reflected. Both Jordan and Josh were tall, lean, Black, and had distinctive jawlines, a particular feature Abbi was certain to point out regularly: "How do you both have such great jawlines!?"

The singular time the two had talked about the possibility of one day having a baby, they'd agreed to look for a donor that resembled Jordan. Josh was admittedly the perfect fit for that. At least Abbi had thought that far. Now, Jordan was only grappling with the sadness of being kept out of the loop this long. Why wouldn't she bring it up? It was an uncertainty that gnawed at their gut with eager teeth.

Yet, there was something almost poetic with the way this had all come out. A sort of synchronicity. Abbi's tears, glistening like the lights all around. Their reflections playing off the window as they looked in at the bumble bee. The beauty of the holiday season, the chill, the way their words condensed in the air and rose, carrying wishes to the heavens.

Jordan could feel something fluttering in the base of their gut, the sort of tug that seemed to say, "Go with it." That was the part of them that loved Abbi so much they'd throw themselves in front of a bullet for her, cliché but one hundred percent true. But, that was only one part of it. Another part wanted to make a big fucking deal out of this.

That other part was deep. Ancestral. Furious. It flared with the recognition that something had been kept from them, that age-old nagging sense of *not being good enough,* of not having a place at the table when decisions seemed to be made about their lives. Was Abbi doing that here? Leaving them out? But, Josh, his skin as dark as theirs, had been in the loop. So could it really be that at all?

Looking down at their hands spread open like starfish, Jordan studied the particular hue of their last two knuckles sticking out of their cut-off gloves. The underside of their fingers, their palms, almost matched Abbi's shoulders after a week at the beach. For a fleeting second, Jordan could imagine the two were equal in all ways, equally privileged. But, as soon as their hands turned over, the sight of the shade of their skin was a harsh inescapable reality.

But, Abbi and Jordan were above all that, right? Always good enough for each other. Abbi didn't care about the color of their skin. She cared that they were making a life together, an almost perfect sort of life, that gave a big middle finger to what median America seemed to think was right or proper. After all, this was the woman who had completely laughed in the face of her parent's insistence that she skip college, settle down with a nice White man, be a homemaker, and birth a couple of kids. If the only part of that vision Abbi ultimately owned was the kids part, at least one, Jordan could live with that.

"Well..."

Abigail was staring up at Jordan expectantly, her eyes grayer in this light than blue. Looking at her had a tendency to make Jordan second guess anything going through their head, at least if that thing was negative.

"I still want to get dinner from *foraged*. And what about your Christmas book?" they asked.

"Does that mean...?"

Jordan sighed, lifting a hand to press against their forehead. The sigh blossomed into a laugh and they felt that sense of synchronicity again. This was crazy. It was rash, sudden, and exactly the sort of thing that could change their lives forever. It was exactly the kind of thing to expect from Abbi. Anything other than the expected.

But, they were an unstoppable force. A power couple. They were queer and unafraid. Bold. Had jobs they loved. Wonderful friends and Abbi's other partner who supported them in every possible way.

And besides, it was an unlikely shot, right? People didn't often get pregnant on the first try, did they? Jordan could think about this in more detail later. So help them, God, though, Abigail's mother Margie was the bane of their Black, butch boi, nonbinary existence, and if this was solely because of her...

"Just tell me," Jordan said, stopping at the sidewalk and reaching a hand out for Abbi to take. "Just tell me 100% for sure, this is what you want."

"This is what I want," Abbi said, her eyes little lakes. "I want to have a baby with you, Jory."

"I don't know what the hell I'm thinking, but if Josh is willing to come spank it into a cup, I'm willing to have a good ol' time with the turkey baster." They flashed the most convincing grin they could, nodded once, then said, "Alright. Let's do it."

NORMALIZING

To make something normal by way of conforming to or reducing to a standard.

JORDAN

They recognized this whole topic of Abbi's Mom, Josh jizzing in a cup, and their entire future as a couple for the treacherous mental territory it was. It was a place where Jordan would overthink and question everything until no joy remained. Instead, Jordan took Abbi's hand as well they could with her thick winter mitts, then steered her on down the sidewalk toward 36th Street. Silence swept up beside them and snuggled in for a comfortable time, until the nagging voice whispering somewhere near the base of Jordan's skull started chattering.

She talked to Josh first.

"So, what kinda book are you thinking?" Jordan asked, interrupting their inner monologue and looking over at their wife's glowing cherry cheeks.

She looked far away, like a girl gone off like a shooting star. Abbi was flying through the speckled cosmos, lost in one of her poetic thoughts, no doubt.

At Jordan's voice again though, she blinked rather dramatically like coming out from a dream and met their fellow wife's eyes.

"Oh... Hmmm... I wonder if Andrea Gibson's got anything new out?"

There had been many a date spent between Jordan and Abbi reading Gibson poems out loud until their sobs choked out their voices.

"Good pick."

Ask if she wants to get a pregnancy book, or a parenting book, maybe? Jordan's mind rattled, but they didn't want to push it right now. They worried the little bit of bitterness was going to come boiling out. They must be reading too much into this.

"But you know me," Abbi said, interrupting Jordan's next tumble of thoughts. "I'm really going to walk in and touch all the books spines one by one and whisper at them until one tells me it's ready to come home."

"Or two... Or five," Jordan said, laughing.

"You're not wrong, Jory my love."

It was a quick walk. The streets of Hampden were bustling with people despite the chill, but the walk to

Atomic Books took less than five minutes. That was one of the lovely things about Hampden. All their favorite stores and eateries were within walking distance. It was dangerous, sometimes, passing the restaurant face that had both indoor seating and an outdoor facing ordering window where you could just wander up and get drinks, a meal, or Abbi's favorite: desserts. Tonight they passed a windowful of cupcakes, cannolis, and doughnuts featuring traditional Christmas colors, all festively iced in reds, greens, and golds. Abbi made a strangled sound of longing.

"Now now, Abs, no ruining your appetite before *foraged*."

Abbi's voice was a long whine as she looked over at Jordan, eyes gleaming with her usual mischievousness. "But, Joooorry, you know I have at least two stomachs, just like that one alien race I designed in that novel series I'm wanting to write."

"I think you really are one of them." Jordan reached out to pinch her side with a crab hand all swathed in wool.

Arriving at the bookstore at last, Jordan held the door for Abbi who skipped in with all the joy of a small child in a toy shop. The store was a bit cramped with all the pre-Christmas shopping, bodies packed in like beads in a tin, everyone dressed in bright winter jackets, knit hats, and jewel-toned sweaters. The books were just as varied, their covers beckoning to them with inviting titles and brilliant designs.

The owner was in tonight, as well as Rob, one of the employees Jordan often got to chatting with about the latest political books. The owner waved to the two of them, and then Abbi was off, a story-seeking missile off honing in on its target. Jordan laughed, turning to Rob who was stocking some books back in the display by the front door.

"Sell outta the window again?" Jordan asked.

"Mmhmm," Rob said, carefully depositing a Black Poetry collection in the display, it's cover crimson. When ze stood back up, ze tucked a strand of blue hair behind zir ear.

"Hey, isn't that the one Abbi and I got like... three times ago?"

"Sure is!" Rob turned toward Jordan and pointed. "Hand me that book over there? One with the gree—yeah, perfect. Thanks. So, anything new and exciting since I saw you last week?" Smirking, ze turned back to wiggle the next book onto one of the wireframe stands.

"Well, Abbi and I are gonna have a baby."

Rob fumbled the book, managing to knock over two of the displays. Ze winced, looking around nervously, but in the noise of shoppers, no one but Jordan had noticed. Ze abandoned the project completely for now, facing Jordan fully. Blue eyes flicked between Jordan, then sought Abbi in the store.

"Woooow," ze said, voice scaling up. "That's exciting! Expensive, probably, but oh em gee, that's rad!"

"Well, if it goes Abbi's way, it won't be expensive at all. She's got a free donor lined up." Jordan shook their head, sucking their lower lip inward.

Rob tapped zir lower lip with the pad of a thumb, brow slightly knit in thought. "Cool. Sweet. Free as it is for the cishets then if all goes well?"

"Sure thing."

"Well, congrats! Let me know if it works. We can always order you some heckin' cute kids books. There are some about pronouns and different types of relationships and all kindsa stuff. You let me know and I'll hook you up!"

"Appreciate it," Jordan said, shooting off two finger guns. "Better go find my wife. Happy Holidays!"

"You too, Jor!"

As they turned back towards the busy shop interior, it struck Jordan how odd it was for them to unload something quite so personal on Rob as that. *Guess I just needed to speak it out loud, try it on...* Rob was definitely not the kind of person that might go leaking such news to the world. Jordan didn't talk to zir outside of the store, they weren't social media friends, and ze had never really spoken to Abbi outside checking her out when she was ready to make a purchase. That often took ages, hence Jordan having gotten to know the clerk. So, it was nothing like announcing it to Dad was going to be, or even co-workers. But, saying it out loud it had felt, well, pretty alright. Not bad. Not like the most over joyous thing in the world, but it could settle and become more. Right now, there was just something irksome about how Abbi had brought the whole thing up. How much did this have to do with her mother?

Margie was the sort of mom who simultaneously doted on and wanted to live through her daughter. Abbi was her baby through and through, and she'd do just about anything to see Abbi as happy, though accepting Abbi was married to a queer Black person was a tough one for her to cheerlead. That much had always been obvious.

Maybe having a child would give their relationship more standing, credibility, or whatever it could be called, in Margie's eyes. She always seemed to believe the couple had one foot each out the door based on Abbi's confusion and glazed expressions whenever they got off the phone: "I don't know why Mom thinks we're not doing well..." she'd say, breathless and nearly in tears.

Wandering through the isles, squeezing past an entire family, several couples, and assorted solo shoppers, Jordan found Abbi in the poetry section, as was typical.

"You got a Christmas book yet?"

Abbi tapped a finger over the spine of three different volumes. "I don't know. Also, there's some really good-looking fiction out right now. The covers are so pretty." Her voice rose to a whispered hiss. "Why do they do that to me?"

"Sucker for a good looking cover," Jordan said.

"I am, and you've got the most handsome cover of any story I've ever read."

Jordan's cheeks warmed a little. Whenever Abbi flirted, it was a thrill up their spine. "You and your words," Jordan said, grinning and leaning down to kiss Abbi. "Get as many books as you want."

Abbi squealed, immediately plucking the three books from the poetry shelf, then scampered off towards the fantasy section like a rat after a snack.

Jordan turned to find the non-fiction section, making themselves paper thin to wiggle between the shelves and peer at the books. Their eyes scanned the titles and stuttered to a stop on "Raising Good Humans: A Mindful Guide to Breaking the Cycle of Reactive Parenting and Raising Kind, Confident Kids." What a damn title. They were surprised that many words could fit on the title. Picking it up and flipping through the pages, they found it was very new, released just that month. Jordan read the back cover, the flaps, then started in on the forward.

The author was a mindfulness instructor. As a social worker, Jordan was familiar enough with mindfulness principals and practices. Breathing in, they snapped the book shut and focused on the feeling of the cover against their palms. Breathing out, they noticed the tension in their body. Pulled tight as a fitted sheet, straining a little at the edges. They were nervous for some reason. Nervous about the idea of being a parent. Nervous about whether Abbi had thought this all through enough. Nervous about how family was going to respond. Above all other anxieties, though, still that worry of why Abbi hadn't brought it up to them first. Before Josh. Had she brought it up to Erica?

The conspirator that took residence in Jordan's head whispered, *Maybe your relationship* isn't *that stable, and you need to stay together for the kids.*

What the hell was that thought? Jordan pushed that one aside swiftly, then wove around the aisles to find Abbi. Their relationship was young, vibrant, and they just needed to be straight with Abs and ask her what was up.

Standing with an armful of at least five books, Abbi gave Jordan a beaming sunshine smile when they finally found her.

"Is five okay?" she asked, her voice pitched up to the point where she sounded all the part a seven-year-old begging for a present.

"Yes, love," Jordan said, taking the books from her hands and stacking them on top of theirs.

"What'd you find?" Abbi bent at the middle to inspect the bottom spine, mostly covered by Jordan's hand now.

"Well..." Jordan could feel heat rising in their throat, lava up a chute. Embarrassment? Anxiety? Anger? It was a weird conglomerate of emotions, made all the more complex by Abbi's big eyes watching. "I figure if we're seriously thinking about this parenting thing, I should start reading up on what to do with kids. I mean, how to be a good parent."

"I was gonna say! You're great with kids. The best. You're so good at your job!"

"Kid therapist is very different than kid parent." Jordan turned to walk toward the counter, ready to be done with the conversation for now. Intense introspection for more than a few minutes sent them spiraling down the slippery slide into suspicion and questions they weren't sure they wanted real answers around.

Plunking the books down, there was a mostly quiet (aside from all the customer's side conversations) span before they were out on the street again. Rob winked at Jordan as they left. Abbi didn't seem to notice. She was still staring at Jordan.

"Jordan, you'll make a great Ren, or Mom, or Dad. Whatever title you decided to go with. Seriously! Do you have doubts?"

Lip sucked through teeth again. Jordan spared a glance at Abbi, trying not to let the nerves show all over their face. "Y-yes?"

"How come?"

"I dunno." Jordan hoisted the paper bag of books up a little higher so they could balance them easier as they walked back to the crosswalk and waited for the light to change. "I've never had kids, and I didn't have siblings. The kids at work don't come home. Do I need to give up beer? Should I stop playing music so loud in the house if there is a baby? I guess no more naked lounging on the sofa."

Abbi laughed, her head tipping back to look up at Jordan as they waited. "You're already doing *this much* overthinking?"

The crosswalk light clicked from the blaring orange hand to the white figure and Jordan immediately bolted across the street.

"Maybe," they said, their voice coming out in a rush of wind.

"Honey, you don't gotta worry!" Abbi said, rushing with her short legs to keep up. "Goddamn, are you running right now?"

"No..." Jordan slowed down, wincing as they heard the hesitation in their own voice. "How sure are you about this?" They'd more or less asked earlier, but their brain was not catching up.

"Very very very. but only if you're on board, too. Even though I'm the one that gets to be all bloaty and gross and you get to look all buff and badass," she said, pouting out her lower lip.

"You'll be gorgeous." Jordan flushed. She would be lovely all glowing with life, a mother tree nurturing a seed.

Abbi blushed, flashed a smile, then tucked her chin into her chest. "Okay, shhhh. You're going to make me overheat."

"It's like 25 degrees out," Jordan said, seeing their own breath cloud in the light of streetlamps and Christmas bulbs.

"Shhh..."

A smirk on their face, Jordan was feeling back to normal. It was sinking in now. This idea. This new beginning. It could be something really special. The kind of thing that would take their lives to a whole new level. Raising a child together, one with two healthy parents who would never tell them what they could or couldn't be in a world that was hopefully getting better with racial issues, environmentalism, and queer rights. Abbi would be even more likely to receive pampering while pregnant, which Jordan would delight in. They'd get to decorate, read books, listen to parenting podcasts. Jordan had always liked the idea of being a really green parent. For fun, they could write a blog together and share their queer parenting feelings.

Maybe it was the right time to have a baby. Besides, what *really* made any particular time "the right time"? No matter when they had a baby, if ever they were going to, it would invite in a type of closeness and teamwork they'd never experienced together before. That would be exciting. They'd agreed that twenty-twenty was going to be their greatest year together, and now it could be the year they started their very own family. That was definitely a once in a lifetime kind of moment worthy of "the best year ever." *Right?*

DREAMING

An experience in waking life containing the characteristics of a dream; or something that satisfies a wish.

Abigail

A family. Abigail stared up at the stars as she walked hand in hand with Jordan. After the flirtatious comment implying she'd be an attractive pregnant woman, they were quiet the rest of the walk home, and that was just as well. Abigail's mind was like a fish tank overstuffed with brightly-hued tropical fish all trying to find a spot amongst the coral. Thoughts flitted in and out, feelings rising and popping like little bubbles on the surface of her experience. The dreams were vivid. Dreams of their future together as a couple and family unit.

There was no small amount of surprise she was noticing right now. It was right in her heart center, a pulsating emerald green all edged in pink that sparkled out over her shoulders and down her arms. Jory was agreeing to try and have a baby! How could it have been so easy? Was it easy? Was Jory over there stewing on something?

Glancing Jory's way, she found her enby wife still smirking, probably mulling over some thought about how extra curvy Abigail would be while pregnant. That was a whole other thing. Would she be able to get pregnant while a bit "overweight?" Okay, doctors would argue that to the death. She was plump. Pleasantly plump as Jor constantly reminded her, and their lovemaking had certainly never indicated she should be otherwise. She shivered delightfully, more little bubbles popping, only this time up her spine at the thought. There was a whole new effervescent wave when she realized they'd likely be doing so tonight if they really went through with this.

Wouldn't that be wild? Amazing? A story for the ages. Maybe that was taking it a little far. What would their child say when they were 20 or so and they finally heard the story of the artificial insemination. Would they laugh? Be appalled? Offended? If Jory and her did a good job raising the kid, they wouldn't care one bit. They'd laugh, roll their eyes, and realize that was just the sort of thing their parents would do. Daydreaming about how good they'd be together as parents only served to make her feel more resolved as it had for the last month or so.

But, still, she was almost shocked at the ease with which Jory was agreeing to all of this. Was their love just that strong? Of course it was.

For as long as she could remember, Abigail was enamored of the idea of being a mother. She didn't care about the husband or the staying at home, but she loved kids which was why she'd pursued a career as a teacher. When she met Jory who also obviously loved kids from their career choice, it had seemed inevitable that eventually they'd have kids. When they'd talked about it, it had always been in passing, with some small amount of excitement; but, they had never seriously discussed the timeline for when or how. What must Jory be feeling with the suddenness of it being brought up?

They dropped the books off in the foyer, then rushed upstairs to change into dinner outfits. Abigail put on a red dress over thick green leggings, touched up her makeup, and pinned up her auburn hair since it was all squashed from her thick knit hat. When she emerged from the bathroom, Jory was wearing a faux-leather vest over a pine green button up, a little reindeer bowtie around their neck, and their other fingerless gloves swapped out for a new pair that better matched the color combination.

"You look handsome as ever," Abigail said, sweeping over to take their hand.

"And you're the most beautiful femme a butch boi could ever ask for, my darling."

As leisurely as was possible given the night's chill, the two walked to *foraged.* bundled in their winter coats. Abigail found herself admiring the Christmas décor all the more now that her secret desire was laid open to her partner. One day, they'd decorate a tree in their living room as a family. The baby would be old enough to open presents. Her and Jor would compete for the most exciting stocking stuffers where the only real winner was their child, but they'd be careful not to make it all about the commercialism. Creating family traditions would be one of the most exciting things they could do. Holiday cocoa making. Decorating the mantle above the fireplace with pinecones and other found things. Maybe they'd make their own Christmas tree ornaments out of upcycled bottles and such, bits of scrap paper, paint, and twigs. The possibilities were limitless, as was Abigail's current sense of joy.

Careful not to trip, Abigail looked over at Jory as they walked, admiring the contours of their face. Gorgeous. She was so glad Josh was a fluke of a physical match, like the two were long lost siblings. Could Jory have ever found a better donor themselves? Abigail somehow doubted it, but still couldn't help but worry there was some prickle of unspoken thing in the air between them.

She commented on the festive décor here and there, pointing out windows on the way to the restaurant, but otherwise just clung to Jordan's arm. When they arrived to *foraged.*, their seat was reserved at their usual spot along the left wall underneath the herb wall.

As soon as they sat and shrugged their coats off, Abigail began playing with the carved wooden mushroom on the table. Her gaze unfocused, her fingers playing over the edges of the figurine, and her mind was suddenly elsewhere. She had that sense of Jordan watching her, picking up the paper menu that Abigail knew they didn't actually need to look at. They always ordered the same thing: the mushroom stew. Even though the menu was as seasonal as changing sometimes every day, the stew seemed to be a staple, and Jordan really liked stability and consistency.

God, this must have been a shock. Completely. Abigail liked to throw some random ideas out there like: "Let's call out of work sick and drive to Salem!" or "How about we call out of family Easter this year and take a road trip!" or "What if we did a camping trip survival style and all we can take with us is a set of matches, a tent, water in a canteen, and some raw vegetables?"

They'd had plenty of random trips and even put themselves in challenging situations just for fun, certainly; but this must be like the biggest and most wild adventure yet, her tossing the idea out there to try getting pregnant the same day she'd announced the thought. It'd make for a good story if it happened, and if it didn't, they could think about it a whole lot more.

There were so many things to think about and plan, but all of that could be figured out along the way. So many straight couples got pregnant by total surprise. They were just, in their own queer way, going to *try* to evoke that same sense of sudden adventure. They'd have just as long as the other people who it was "random" for to make a nursery, learn more about parenting, gather the appropriate supplies, agree on names and décor and...

"Whatcha thinking about over there, Babbi?" Jordan asked, breaking Abigail out of her daydreams.

"Oh, I'm thinking about the nursery," she said, titrating the rush in her head down to only that. "We can change that spare room across from ours."

The waiter came over, his Deathly Hallows tattoo showing prominently on his arm. Abbi smiled up at him.

"We'll take a cornbread to start," she said. "And then I'll have the carrot salad and the roasted sunchokes."

The waiter looked to Jordan, probably expecting what they were about to say.

"Mushroom stew for me. And a bottle of the rosé."

Chuckling, the waiter turned back to the kitchen.

"Anyway, nursery," Abbi said.

"Do you have a theme idea already?" Jordan asked.

"Maybe something off whatever their Zodiac sign ends up being. We could base it around their element, maybe!"

Jordan smirked. "You love your Zodiac shit, don't you."

"Mhm! But, not as much as I love you."

"I love you, too, Abbi."

The waiter delivered the wine and the cornbread at the same time, pouring each of them with a flourish. The rest of the restaurant faded, woody browns and moss greens a haze of hue and the patrons a blur. Jordan appeared to study every edge of Abbi's form as she moved to cut a piece of cornbread. As she moaned softly around the flavor. Sipped the wine. Cheeks colored to pink roses. She sighed, meeting Jordan's golden eyes with a little private smile.

"You're looking at me all thoughtful, again," Abigail said. "Like I'm the only thing in the world."

"And so you are..." Jordan paused briefly, their thick brows drawing closer together. "You're really, really sure of this, then, huh?"

Abigail felt her stomach do a complex series of little spins and dips before she nodded. "Yeah. I think, maybe, I've never been so sure of anything in my life." No. That was wrong. Her lips curled up around the corners like a drying leaf, a slight smile before she amended her statement. "Never so sure of anything since I met you, that is. I've been thinking about it non stop lately and I'm ready. Ready to try. It's exciting, really..."

Looking down at the crumbing piece of bread, Abigail felt suddenly as if she might be overcome with tears. As means of distracting herself, she lapped up some of the pumpkin butter with it, then chewed a long moment. When she swallowed, she gulped down the wave of emotion, too.

"The way I see it, Jor, you're going to be an absolutely stellar parent whether now or in the future. We're in a really good place, I think. And, I mean, let's be fair. My uterus is more or less a ticking time bomb, isn't it? Sometimes couples tell themselves 'Oh, when this happens or that happens,' and before they know it, they're fifty and it's past their time."

Nodding along with the explanation, Jordan watched her speak, eyes hovering on her lips. There was a flicker of a frown for a second as Abigail implied her age, but she knew she was right. She was already in her 30s, and although in pretty good health, all the warnings seemed to indicate by 35 you might as well give up. Even if that wasn't entirely true, she felt that weight of invisible pressure on her always. The sort of now or never. Lately, it had risen to be so loud, a constant shout in the back of her mind, that she was actually surprised she hadn't burst with the desire to get pregnant already.

"I get all that," Jordan said. "The part I don't get... The part that's bothering me..."

They chugged a gulp or two of wine.

Abigail leaned forward, her glass cradled between her knit fingers, her expression shifting from wistful to worried. So there *was* something in the air between them. She wasn't wrong. "What's bothering you, Jory?"

When Jordan spoke, the words seemed to tumble right out. There was an edge in their voice, a hesitance, that seemed to imply they didn't want to sap Abigail's joy. But, there was an obvious pain there, a sting from some barb.

"I'm just a little upset you talked to Josh before me. Did you talk to Erica, too?" They looked down at the table quickly to hide the shame that washed over their face.

"Oh, Jory..." Abigail actually half-choked on a laugh, a strangled one, the repressed tears coming up and over again. She normally wasn't the emotional one, yet here they were, and somehow, Jory was the stoic one.

With her free hand, Abigail reached across the table and met Jordan's, pressing her smaller fingers in between each of Jordan's so that their hands created a striped pattern. They'd made this on their first official date. Ebony fingers alternating with pale peach ones, both palms flat against the table. It was effortless for them to interlace like this now.

"No, I haven't talked to Erica about it yet," she said. "Or told Mom I am thinking about it, either. The only person I talked to was Josh to see if it'd be an option if he agreed to it. Otherwise, we'd have to find a donor through a clinic and that could take a long time. I told you today because..." She sat the wineglass down on the table, licked her fingers clean of the butter, then reached out for Jordan's other hand. "Because I've been kinda scared you'd say no, and I've been putting it off because it's something important to me. I was sort of planning on bringing it up after the holidays, but something tonight about that bumble bee ornament, I have no fucking clue why, but it just yanked the words right out of me."

Jordan visibly relaxed, blowing a breath out from between pursed lips. "Okay. So, to be clear, you actually told me before you were going to tell me anyway?"

With a nod, Abbi gave an apologetic smile. "Yeah... Actually... I was thinking of maybe doing a PowerPoint or a spreadsheet..."

At that, Jordan couldn't help but burst with giggles, fingers tightening in the pattern on the table. When they braided together like this, it always felt like neither's fingers were their own and they were one tapestry stitched together.

"Remember our first date-date?" Abigail asked, wiggling her fingers against Jordan's to nestle them down even more.

"Of course. Every bit of it."

The date had taken place not too far from here at the American Visionary Art Museum in Baltimore. It was an incredible building filled with thought-provoking exhibits, full of light, hope, and also sorrow. They'd gone in the morning and not come out until dinner time, talking about what seemed like every single piece.

"So you remember the moment when we put our fingers together for the first time like this."

Jordan laughed, shaking their head, eyes wide. "Mhm. I was just thinking about it."

They'd grabbed an early breakfast and within the first few minutes of meeting up, they'd joined hands on the table, palms flat just like now. Abigail's smaller fingers had worked their way down between Jordan's spread on the table. It had been an invitation she'd taken almost immediately, not needing to ask for clarification.

Grinning, Abigail bit her lower lip at one side, her eyebrows lifting. "Mind meld is as strong as ever, I see. That moment we shared was just... I looked down at our black and white hands. It was like my fingers fit right into yours like little nooks built just for me. Like zipping up a zipper or pulling corset strings. It wasn't quite a perfectly straight stripe pattern, but, when are we ever straight?

"It was a weave, some overlaps, some little inconsistencies, but for some reason, my brain decided we were perfect stripes, perfectly symmetrical, and it became my visual symbol for us, you know?" When she pulled back one hand in order to take a sip of her wine, it was like pulling away from comfort and ease; she wanted to go right back.

Both of them reached for the cornbread at the same time, fingers bumping. They giggled, then split the piece in half.

"I spent the rest of the date looking for striped patterns in the art, signs that we were meant to be together. I found them hidden in so many art pieces, little illusions of the paint strokes sometimes. Other times boldly there. In tapestries. In the wood on benches. Everything was striped like our fingers... Then, we came up to that one painting, the sort of surrealist one. A table set with flowers, roses, and two plates, each heaped with glistening fruit. There was a striped cloth spread over a table, dripping down into a fog of color, the black and white swirling into a vortex. I remember my brain couldn't really make out what I was seeing because it was all like, 'Stripes!' And, 'Woah, the colors,' and 'Fruit would make for a weird romantic dinner!' And then, you just looked at me and said—"

"It's a dinner for us," Jordan said. "And the cloth looks like our fingers did earlier."

Still with slightly misty eyes, Abigail bowed her head. "Exactly, and I thought to myself, 'Holy shit, they read my mind,' sort of anyway, and I knew in that moment that you were overlapped with me in more than body, but mind and spirit, too."

"Then I kissed you," Jordan said, smirking.

"You did. Read the room just right."

Abigail wanted to lean across the table and kiss them then, but their food was ready and, logistically it was impossible anyway.

The food smelled and looked as divine as ever, herbaceous and vibrant. Naturally, Jordan didn't wait a moment before grabbing their spoon and diving into the mushroom stew

Abigail picked up her fork, spearing a carrot. "So, the reason I bring that story up is I've never had any doubts about doing anything in life with you, not a single time since that first moment we were in each other's heads. We're a pair of stripes. We complete each other's pattern."

Jordan swallowed, and Abigail got a distinct empathic punch that for some reason, Jordan was swallowing down some little swell of guilt along with their stew. "Yeah... We are like that, Abs."

"You okay?" Abigail asked.

"Yeah. Great, actually," Jor said.

Their smile seemed convincing enough as Abigail studied it, and the feeling in her stomach was gone. So, rather than dredging up whatever was going on in Jor's often overthinking head, she took another bite of her food and wiggled in her chair.

"Speaking of nursery themes, though," Jor said, "If not your prior suggestion, maybe we could do bumble bees with black and yellow stripes."

"Oh that's heckin' cute," Abbi said, tears renewed.

"You're cute," Jordan said, reaching across and wiping at her eye.

"You're the best, most supportive partner a girl could dream of, you know."

Really, Jordan was quite possibly the most supportive possible partner in the world. Maybe even to a fault. Abigail couldn't, for all her fantasy-filled mind, imagine a partner more suited to her.

"Thanks, Babbi. You're the most gorgeous, smart, inspiring gal an enby could dream of, too."

Abigail smiled over the rim of her wine glass, her eyes flaring up at the corners. "I guess dreams do come true, don't they?"

"You're the proof."

CONCEPTION

A beginning.

JORDAN

Dinner, a bottle of wine, and a slightly tipsy walk to admire the Christmas lights later, Abbi and Jordan found Josh leaning in the frame of the front door to their house. The shadows of the evening made it hard to work out his expression.

Abbi lifted up a brown paper bag, holding it out for him while she fished clumsily with a mitted hand for the keys in her pocket. "Here. We got takeout for you."

"*foraged.*? Damn, that's some fancy ass shit right there," Josh said, finally coming fully into view as he stepped off the postage stamp porch and out into the streetlights. He walked a bit like a cat, each step fluid and graceful. "You were really serious, eh, Abbi?"

"I was." When she winked at Josh, Jordan felt that momentary knot at their core, but it was gone about as soon as Abbi rolled her eyes and Josh cackled.

Abbi handed off the bag of gourmet roast chicken with potatoes to Josh, then managed to unlock the door. As soon as they were in the foyer, she cast off her puffy jacket and mitts, then moved with singular purpose towards the kitchen cabinet to fish for something inside. After a moment, she returned with two bottles of wine, a turkey baster, a specimen cup, and a sleeve sex toy.

"Wow." This time it was Josh and Jordan that spoke in unison.

"You've really been thinking about this, Abs," Jordan said, beyond amused at this point.

"I don't have to use that sleeve thing, right?" Josh said, a note of disgust in his voice.

Abbi laughed until she had to sit down at the round dining table halfway between the kitchen and living room. She plunked the wine bottles down, waving a hand that non-verbally indicated Jordan should retrieve wine glasses, and tried to reel the giggles in. A hand went to her stomach, clutching over her dress as if she hurt, but she couldn't stop laughing.

"I saw it in Sugar when I was there the other day and just thought... Maybe you could use help. You know... Not from a person. I don't know!" The giggle fit started anew.

Jordan shook their head. "You are some piece of work, Abbi, my love." They set three wine glasses down, then went back into the kitchen to get a bottle opener. Uncorking the first vino with a deliberately dramatic series of movements, they poured each of them a glass as Josh sat down with his dinner.

"Okay, but... I enjoy a well-thought-out plan," Abbi said.

Although they knew now that this was not something she'd pondered over in the dark for a long time, that she'd been nervous, scared to have a dream denied, Jordan couldn't help but wish they'd found out sooner. Been able to share in all of this with Abbi. Still, it made sense.

"To Abbi's plans!" Jordan said, opting for the supportive route that suited them best. Lifting their wine glass, they said in an announcer's voice, "To Josh mustering the will to beat his meat so I can shove a turkey baster in my wife's—"

"JORY!" Abbi roared, losing it again. She devolved into tearful mirth on the table, her arms folding over her head as her face planted into the placemat.

"You all have issues," Josh said, though his features betrayed him. He was trying, and succeeding not at all, to keep the smile smoothed to a flat line. Soon, he was laughing with them. "I can't deny it, ya'll couple goals. Except for the sex part."

The sex part was the best part sometimes. Nah, not really. Everything in their relationship was the best part. They'd never really fought, except play arguments about things like who should do the laundry and why or when was an appropriate bedtime when they really wanted to binge-watch a new drama on Netflix. They agreed on just about everything. Enjoyed listening to music together. Went out on dates all the time and tried new food. They were getting healthier together, changing up their lifestyle. Jordan was drinking less. Abbi was binging less sugar. They adored their home and city. They loved their jobs and talked every night about work without tiring of each other. Even on days they felt exhausted and too worn to speak, there was unfathomable comfort in simply snuggling and dozing off in each other's arms. While the world around them seemed to be full of relationships wrought with drama and disagreement, they were on the same page even if it took a little bit more communication to make sure.

When they, at last, slipped into the bedroom with Josh's specimen cup in hand and, indeed, a turkey baster, Jordan was met with the sight of about fifty candles all lit in the room. It was warm from the flames, but Abbi had taken care to crack a window and a few tendrils of the night's crisp air were working their way in.

Abbi was posed on top of their maroon sheets, dressed in a silky white robe, open to expose the matching bralette and thong set beneath. Jordan's jaw slackened. Suddenly, they were profoundly aware through the creep of heat over their thighs and inward that there was something incredibly provocative about the idea of trying to get Abbi pregnant.

Never would they have given serious thought to being the one to inseminate Abbi; they'd have assumed it was a thing they needed to go to a doctor to do if and when they were ready. But, here they were, though the tools might be far from sexy, with their sumptuous wife laid before them and all the means to start a family at their disposal.

Was this what it felt like to be a cis man?

No way. This is what it felt like to be queer, creative, free, and on top of that, they more than knew how to pleasure a thick, wanting woman. Definitely not a claim many cis men seemed to be able to make.

Setting down the insemination kit, Jordan undid the clasps on their vest, unbuttoned their top, and loosened their tie. Without a moment's hesitation, they were down to boxer briefs and socks in such short time all Abbi managed to do was roll onto her back and spread her legs.

"Apparently saliva can kill sperm," Abbi said, running a hand up her own side. "Sooo, you'll have to get me all worked up some other way."

"I think I can arrange that." Jordan tried really hard not to think about the substance sitting on the bedside table. Instead, they kissed their way up from Abbi's feet to her thighs, kissing overtop her panties where they covered the bits Jordan would normally lick and nibble at. Abbi shuddered, her skin flaring with heat and goosebumps. "Gotta get you all worked up so I can slip that baster in real deep."

The two of them devolved into more snickering, but it abated quickly as Jordan sealed their mouth around one of Abbi's nipples, the silk between their teeth.

Doing their best attempt at some sort of dirty talk (Abbi liked that *a lot*), Jordan said, "I bet you can't wait to feel me inside you, baby... Can't wait for me to knock you up."

Abbi whimpered and spread her legs wide open, her head turning so that her cheek rested against the pillow. Her skin was flushed head to toe. One hand on a breast, Jordan moved the other down to slip into Abbi's panties and found her so wet their fingers slipped right between her folds.

"Shit, babe," they said, feeling themselves throb. "Seems I really didn't need to use the old warm-up routine."

Lips pressed tight, Abbi looked at Jordan with an expression so needy they couldn't help but be smug. It was time to give their wife what she wanted.

It was well after midnight when Jordan and Abigail finally began dozing, their naked limbs intertwined like milky moonlight and bronze. Jordan was all hard edges and lines, their chest flat and scarred. Abigail was circles upon circles, soft like a plush toy, and just as nice to hold. There was an unpalatable smell in the air, like dampness and bleach—a scent Jordan had gratefully never smelled before. If Josh's sample took, which they both hoped and didn't hope it would, they'd never have to try at this insane sort of scheme again.

JOY

The emotion brought about by well-being, success, or good fortune, or by the prospect of possessing what one desires.

JORDAN

Abbi got up early on Christmas morning to make coffee, promising Jordan breakfast in bed. She'd delivered with a wonderful array of fresh muffins, sautéed spinach, hash browns, and tofu scramble with a mug of fresh hot coffee and some berries on the side. When Abigail sat down on the edge of the bed, the first thing Jordan noticed was she wasn't drinking coffee herself. They said nothing of it, assuming Abbi was playing it safe just in case their tryst with Josh's splocge had been successful. Jordan shivered, a creeping sense of the strangeness that had been that evening coming back fresh. Rather than get tangled in that thought, though, they sat up, gave Abbi a long, lingering kiss, and traced her brows with a fingertip.

"You're the best. Happy Christmas."

"No, you," Abbi said, thrumming with energy. "I love you, and Merry Christmas."

After breakfast, Jordan stacked all the dishes and took them into the kitchen to wash. Humming as they turned the water on, they looked up to see the Lesbian Book balanced on the windowsill.

They took it down, feeling the sleek black cover a moment before they flipped open to the latest entry marked with a ribbon.

December 25th, 2019

A buzzing stirs in my belly
And you're to be a Renny

Jordan stopped reading immediately, their face suddenly radiating heat and numb in tandem. They couldn't feel their lips, and was the floor flat? Straight? The title "Renny" was the term they'd long ago said they'd use if they were a parent. Ren, short for paRENt, was a nice gender-neutral term, but they never expected it to actually be something they'd use.

They were brought back to reality when a spray of water pelted them in the chest, ricocheting off a dish that must have slipped. They quickly turned the water off, then dragged their eyes back to the page, a whirring starting up in their head and heart.

The results are come
We are done
We've nailed it in a single shot

OK – that was the shittiest poem I've ever written, but I can't help myself. :D We did it! We did it on the first try! Now you never have to handle sperm again. Aren't you happy? Oh my GOD. Happy Christmas, Renny! You're going to be a great parent, and I'm so happy you decided to do this with me, even if it seemed like it was on a whim. You're the most supportive partner a gal like me could ever hope for, and it's so hard to believe once upon a time I tried to live a fake cishet life on behalf of my parents. But, this queer life is perfect, and we're going to be amazingly GAY parents together. It won't be what my mom wants exactly, but it's as good as she's ever going to get because you are the only person on this planet I'd ever wanna have a baby with. <3 I love you sooo much. – Your Babbi

Jordan turned around slowly to see Abbi standing in the kitchen's archway with an early read pregnancy test in her hand. She waved it slightly, then immediately devolved into tears.

Jordan tossed the notebook on the counter and went to her quickly, wrapping Abbi in a huge hug.

"I love you, too, Abs. Oh my God," they whispered, their lips pressed into the top of Abbi's auburn hair. "Oh... My God. It happened."

"Mmhm." Abbi's face was pressed into the plain of Jordan's chest, dampening it with her tears. "It's really happening."

"How are you feeling?"

Abbi leaned back to look up at Jordan. "I don't even know. I thought I'd feel more excited, but I am honestly just amazed? Like, I didn't think it'd actually happen the first time. I wasn't really tracking my cycle, to be honest, and I didn't think you'd go along with it, and..."

"Yeah, it's a lot to take in," Jordan said. Their eyes were unfocused, and they reached around to touch something solid. The doorframe was closest.

It was a lot. It was surprising they'd gone along with it. It was almost a fluke of the fates that it all happened the way it did. Josh being willing to go along with it and having the perfect donor and it happening so swiftly and seamlessly. It must be meant to be, Jordan figured, accepting it right there in the moment and pulling Abbi closer. They smiled, feeling their own tears rising despite all their worries.

"You're going to be the world's best Momma. I mean it."

"Thanks, Jory. Thanks for being willing to do this."

That was the kicker, wasn't it? This was for Abbi, no doubt. Not for them.

But, it could be.

They knew parenthood had never been entirely off the table. In fact, prior to this, Abbi seemed more anti-parenthood than Jordan overall. Jordan simply had never wanted to be pregnant, but that didn't mean they didn't enjoy the idea of kids. They worked with kids as a career and found it rewarding. But, it was also endlessly sad because many of the kids they saw at the hospital were already at the ends of their lives, ill with chronic conditions and unexpected diseases. Having a child of their own had the potential to be so beautiful and the exact opposite of their daily experience.

"This means no cats, I guess. We have no way to know how they'd get along with the baby," Jordan said. "But, babies can talk eventually, and that's pretty cool."

Abbi leaned back to stare up into Jordan's face. Her nose wrinkled a bit as her lips pursed. "No caaaats," she whined. "But, I really was hoping for cats soon now that we're all settled in. But, you have a good point. Are you disappointed?"

"No, Babbi, I'm happy for us."

"Really?"

"Yes, really." They tilted Abbi's face up with their thumb and forefinger, bowing to kiss her tenderly. "Like I said, you're going to be a great Momma. And I'm going to be the most stylin' Renny ever. This kid is going to be too cool for school."

"Oh God. Do we want to homeschool?" Abbi said.

Jordan chuckled. "You're always thinking like eight years ahead, aren't you? Except those times when you're not. We'll talk about it when we get there, sweets. No need to rush. First, you get to fight off morning sickness and feeling bloated all the time." Jordan shivered again.

"Fair enough." Abbi sighed, but then shifted from resigned to excited within another moment's breath. "Do you want to find out our due date and stuff? And I... I'd call an OBGYN to schedule, but I guess they're probably on vacation for Christmas. Maybe they're open tomorrow... What day is tomorrow, even? Thursday. Yes! They should be open tomorrow."

"Do you already have an OBGYN picked out for your pregnancy, then?" Jordan asked, feeling quite amused at totally calling out Abbi's constant pre-planning of all the little, typically insignificant things.

"Yep. Dr. Diaz in downtown B-more. I hear she's pretty great."

"And yes, I'd like to find out the due date," Jordan added before Abbi could fly off on yet another tangent.

"Yeah, let's do that!" Abbi turned, jaunting through the living room and up the stairs toward their home office.

Jordan followed after pouring another cup of coffee, appreciating the warmth in their hands on the crisp Christmas morning. Once in the office, they sat down in their chair and rolled over to Abbi, careful not to slosh their mug.

Abbi was already rapidly typing and clicking, pulling up a due date calculator on Google.

"Date of conception..." Click, click, click. "Looks like we're probably due around September 7th, 2020. That makes our little bean a..."

Another Google search. "A Virgo! Well, let's hope someone in this household is one day organized. They won't get that from you or me for sure."

She swept a hand around at their messy little office. Abbi was working on two novel concepts and had poetry pages littered everywhere. Jordan side-eyed their own loose stack of sheet music and lyrics for various songs they were writing on their guitar. The shelves in the space were crammed full of music books, fiction, and a few psychology titles leftover from their grad school days.

Abbi, looking like she might vibrate right out of her skeleton said, "I'm literally never going to finish a novel now! I'm going to be too busy doting on the baby like I've been too busy doting on you for the past few years."

There was a fleeting worry that maybe they wouldn't get as much of Abbi's attention with a baby in the mix, but that vanished quickly as more images of them doing family activities like beach vacations and craft nights rose to replace the fear.

Scooting in closer, Jordan pressed their lips to Abigail's forehead and said, "Well, I'm gonna dote on you no matter what, Momma. So you better prepare yourself for all the doting in the world. You and this beeb ain't got a single clue just how lovey-dovey heart eye-emoji I can get."

"No? I mean, I've seen you get pretty lovey-dovey. Your proposal was pretty extra after all..."

"You. Ain't. Seen. NOTHING!" Jordan said, emphasizing each word as they reached out with lightning bolt fingers to tickle Abbi's sides.

Abbi squealed and kicked, playing into their usual game. She was all smiles, vibrant with life this morning, and Jordan wasn't sure they'd ever loved her more.

"I want to do something to celebrate!" Jordan said, after a round of jubilant lovemaking.

"That wasn't celebration enough?" Abbi asked, sitting up and grabbing a bedside towel to dab at her brow with.

"I wanna pamper you!" Jordan slid off the bed and started pulling on clothes. "I think I'm going to make dinner rather than us just getting Chinese."

That was their tradition, after all. Chinese on Christmas Day.

"I can come with you!"

Jordan shook their head, lifting a hand. "No, no. You celebrate that you're growing a little life nugget in you, and watch some of your favorite shows and lounge. Today is all about you, baby."

"Which baby are you referring to now?" Abbi asked, giggling until her cheeks were rosy.

"Mmm. Both of you, I suppose!"

After assuring Abbi she should take the day to relax in whatever way felt best, Jordan fretted over how to make a special experience to remember it by. They supposed wine was probably not the best bet now, and it was Christmas day, so many of the restaurants and stores were closed. Their brain was abuzz with a thousand bursting dreams now, what all they could do with the nursery, how they could be a team through it all, and how they'd best pamper Abbi so she could have the best pregnancy imaginable. Jordan could still barely wrap their mind around the news. Aside from the excitement, there was a silent triumph, too, in not needing to smell jizz anytime soon, and they were reasonably sure Josh would be thrilled as well.

As a celebration of the new life they were creating, Jordan decided to cook dinner that night: homemade veggie sushi. Shortly after tucking Abbi in with a cup of rooibos tea, a blankie, and some Christmas morning cartoons, Jordan drove to the local Asian market. They were practically floating above the earth, and everything that had seemed mundane before on their own seemed suddenly vibrant. They bought the most colorful seaweed, exotic mushrooms, peppers, avocado, sweet potatoes, and carrots they could find. The rest of the afternoon, they marinated, chopped, steamed, and cooked, making the sticky sushi rice to the best of their ability and then rolling up a dozen different combos.

Exhausted, but thrilled, Jordan drew Abbi into the kitchen once everything was complete.

It wasn't by any means the most elaborate display Jordan had ever pulled off, but they felt pretty pleased. The round dining table with its stool seats was set with only two chairs which were scooted side by side. The whole kitchen was lit by Christmas lights, including some strands wound carefully around the platters of sushi on the table. They'd selected plain soft white lights for the table, choosing to highlight the look of the sushi, and it had worked. It was easy to see the intensity of the vegetables within the rice, shining little jewels of flavor, all-natural beauty. The silver platters, some thrift store finds they'd gotten long ago with the hopes of entertaining, gleamed with the reflections of the lights so that the meal seemed somewhat otherworldly. Jordan had set out some flowers, the last they could find at the market, displaying some in a squat glass vase and others amongst the carefully crafted rolls.

Eyes wide as cucumber slices, Abbi looked between the feast and Jordan. Her mouth opened and closed a few times, her expression shifting in each moment with a new emotion. "I don't even know what to say... I know how much hard work it is to make sushi from scratch and... Oh my God, no wonder the house smelled so good," she said, grinning. "It was torture staying upstairs, you know."

Abbi threw her arms around Jordan's shoulders, pulling them tight in. Jordan loved this feeling, the way their wife's soft form pressed against all their wiry muscles and bones.

"You're an incredible wife, you know," Abbi said, her lips against Jordan's ear.

Shivering at the feeling of Abbi's breath, Jordan wrapped their arms around her waist and leaned back to look at her. "And you are the best wife for this wife."

Glancing at the food again, Abbi's stomach gave an audible and timely grumble. "Can we maybe eat now?"

With a laugh, Jordan disentangled from the embrace, then moved to pull out a chair for her. "M'lady."

With a bit of drama, Abbi gave a little bow, then slid into the chair. She shimmied her bottom down into the seat. "Why thank you, Lordy Jor."

For the first few minutes of the meal, Jordan simply fed Abbi from a pair of their favorite chopsticks. The set was replete with a pink and white floral pattern on metal, the pair they'd gotten in a shop in DC on a trip down to see an art show about cherry blossoms. The print was starting to fade with use, but they always gravitated toward using them whenever they could. Tonight was definitely the right kind of occasion.

Taking a few bites between feeding Abbi, Jordan relaxed into the state of watching and observing their wife, admiring the way her cheeks moved when she chewed and the way her eyes shut slightly with delight. It was easy to admire her. Easy to get lost in her little expressions of bliss.

"I feel..." Jordan said, plopping another sushi piece in Abbi's mouth, "I feel like I've never been this happy? But, like... It's also almost out of reach. It's unreal, I guess. Obviously, it's been pretty sudden, you know. We talked about it. We did it. It's been ten days or something, and here we are."

In truth, that was exactly how it had been. They talked about it. Made their attempt. Then went on living as if nothing happened. That's how Abbi was, often. Blunt and to the point about whatever, then moving on without a care for the outcome. Obviously, she cared about this outcome, but Jordan suspected she didn't speak about it because it was so fragile and tentative, and she wasn't one to hope too much.

Abbi nodded, her eyes flickering down to watch Jordan dip the next roll in soy sauce. "I get it. I know I took a pregnancy test and it was positive. And while you were gone I took two more. Also positive. But, until I have a blood test or a heart monitor or something, it's not going to feel entirely real. So, I get it."

"Still," Jordan said, voice coming out in a rush of breath. "I haven't felt this happy since our wedding day. And that was the best day of my life. I imagine the next best day after this will be when we're holding that baby in our arms, giving them a name. And then every birthday after that..."

Eyes swimming, Abbi nodded. Jordan caught a tear with a knuckle as it rolled down Abbi's face.

"I haven't cried happy tears, I mean, aside from the laughter ones, in a while either," she said. "Thank you, Jory, for being so supportive. I am so, so happy, but the biggest reason is that I'm doing this with you. You're my safe place in this big wide world, my light, and my wonder. I can't imagine a life without you."

Jordan felt the mini-gut punch. It was soft. Muffled. But, still set their own enthusiasm to pause for a moment. *I can't imagine a life without you.* They'd felt the same way about their mother, but she had passed when Jordan was only 15. Looking across the table at Abbi, Jordan swept a hand up to cup her cheek, thumb brushing over her temple. A life without Abbi would be empty, drained of all its colors and sounds.

No matter what, Abbi had to be okay. So long as that was true, Jordan would be fine. Come what may, they could handle anything else the world could throw at them. Nothing else could take away their joy.

SETTLING

The act of coming to rest; becoming fixed,
resolved or established.

Abigail

Abigail was not an anxious person by nature. Or at least, she didn't think so. Cautious was maybe a better word. Sensible? Farsighted? That one seemed to taste bad in her mouth, so she shrugged it off with all the other slurry of words that typed their way through her mind with clanging keys. With effort, she drew her attention back to the road.

When finally she pulled up to the pregnancy clinic, she was thankful they weren't closed. So many places had opted to shut down for the entire time between Christmas and New Year's Day, but it was the 30th and a Monday, so she was lucking out. However, getting the results of the blood test back could take up to 48 hours, they'd told her, though often less. She hoped it could be a quick turnaround for her sanity, and for the surprise she hoped would be a good way to start the incoming new year. Twenty-twenty! It was going to be the best year ever! She wanted to feel secure in telling everyone: Her family and her other partner Erica.

Abbi grabbed her purse from the passenger seat, trying to ignore the shaking of her hands. "You're not nervous," she told herself aloud, lifting her chin up and closing her eyes for a moment to steel herself. Then, she was out into the frosty morning and into the office.

Greeted by pistachio ice cream walls and paintings of landscapes, Abigail walked to the check-in window and filled her name out on the clipboard. She didn't need to do any paperwork since she'd grabbed the intake forms online. After finding a seat, she fiddled with her purse strap, picking at the fraying bits of string and faux leather that was flaking. Flaking like her own inner sense of self. Was she really ready to be a mother? Had she really expected when she brought everything up to get an affirmative response from her wife right away? All the second-guessing was seeping into her marrow now, filling her bones to the brim with self doubt.

"Abigail Robins?" a voice said from a nearby doorway.

Abigail jumped out of her seat, waving a hand awkwardly at the nurse. "That's me."

"I'm Tara. Come on back. We'll get your vitals and a few other things, then draw your blood. How are you feeling?"

Abigail gulped down the nervous titter that she knew would threaten her voice. She was a competent, educated woman, a soon-to-be mother. She could handle herself in a doctor's office. Shoving the fears and wonderings about her own choices into a mental shoebox, she clamped the lid shut and tossed it into the darkest corner of her mind.

"I'm doing great!" she said, following the nurse into an eggshell-colored corridor, the walls bare save for arrows pointing the way back out to the lobby. There was nothing to focus on, no pretty pictures to daydream and make up stories about, so she watched the nurse's footsteps and marched behind dutifully.

"Let's get your weight. You're how tall?"

"Five foot five," Abigail said, stepping up onto the scale.

Tara's eyes flicked over Abigail, then down to the blaring red 235 on the scale, and her pen went flying, scribbling a note. "Alright, just this way. Do you know the possible date of conception?"

Abigail internally snickered. Possible. There was literally only one possibility. "We would have conceived the night of December 15th."

"When would be the first day of your missed period?"

73

"Honestly, I'm not 100% sure. I didn't really track too well given I had no risk of getting pregnant until I made the choice."

The nurse glanced down at the chart she had printed, then gave a knowing wink. "Got it. Best guess?"

"Probably yesterday?"

Tara nodded with another scratch at her clipboard. "Let's get you set up for the blood draw. It's a quick one. Any issues with blood work?"

"Nope," Abigail said, proud of her own unwavering sense of confidence when it came to medical work. She'd been pretty healthy throughout her life, despite what people tended to think based on her weight.

Sitting down in a chair in a room full of blank cabinets, Abigail watched as the nurse got out everything needed for the phlebotomist's work. Despite opening half a dozen doors and drawers, Tara located everything with efficiency, placed the items on the silver tray beside the chair, and then left the room.

Alone, Abigail looked around at the mostly empty room. Her eyes flicked back and forth, up and down, left and right. Chair and cabinets. Printed off posters reminding others to cover their mouths when they cough. Chair and cabinets. The same signs with words that lost all meaning after the fifth read-through. Chair and cabinets.

She became intimately aware of her heartbeat. It was strong. Far louder in her ears than usual. The florescent lights of the small space left her feeling exposed, laid bare for all to see the doubts rising again. *Breathe*, she told herself. *Just breathe.*

Summoning the image of her mother, Abigail found a little solace. Mom was always great at doctor's visits, reassuring little Abigail that everything was going to be alright, consoling her when things hurt, and offering her treats for her suffering when things were less comfortable than promised.

Once, Abigail had fallen from a bike and broken her ankle while riding around with a few boys in their neighborhood. Abigail had somehow managed, perhaps through the sheer power of shock and adrenaline, or more her typical self-protective nature, not to cry in front of the boys. Helped by two of them back home, she'd cried only when Mom began to offer reassurances, getting her to the car and driving to the hospital. There, she hadn't scolded Abigail overly much for her "boyish" behaviors. Abigail was a girly girl, after all, and Mom probably thought and approved of the idea that she was just trying to impress the boys. Regardless, she'd been very good through all of Abigail's medical visits, whether for ear infections, colds, allergies, or even her weight.

That was the only little mark in Mom's score. Despite flawless bloodwork and "clean bills of health" from every doctor or specialist they went to, Mom was worried about Abigail's weight. She'd always been on the thicker side for her height and seemed resistant to weight loss. That's just how her body was. The sweet spot for her was not thin; it was voluptuous. Mom had finally shut down her criticisms when Abigail landed a modeling job for a upcoming inclusive fashion company when she was in her 20s, proving that big was *also* beautiful.

Settling on the memories of her mother offering reassurance only reminded her of why she'd wanted to get pregnant in the first place. After Thanksgiving dinner, Mom had given her a big hug while Jory ran around to gather their things.

As she rubbed Abigail's back with a palm, she said, "You know, it's so good to see you happy, love. It's the best thing in the world. All I ever wanted for my babygirl was to know she was happy, and I know I've had my worries. But, you're full of life when you're around Jordan." She pulled back from the embrace to look over her daughter. "I'm glad. I'm glad someone sees you for the beautiful girl you always were."

"Aw, Ma," Abigail said. She almost couldn't look at her. Mom always doted on her, but this was a lot.

"The only greater gift would be a grandbaby, I think," Mom said, then turned to grab Abigail's coat from the rack without another word.

In Jory's career as a therapist, they'd experienced many of what described a phenomenon known as the "Door Knob Confession." This was when a client was on their way out of the office and right as their hand touched the door knob, they'd drop something big that ideally should have been processed in the session. Something that came with an emotional punch. "Oh by the way, my sister died," or "I've been feeling hollow, like I don't really exist anymore." These moments were allegedly universal for therapists and often frustrating, but there was little one could do when the next client was sitting in the waiting room.

"Mom," Abigail said, "That's a big..."

It was at that moment Jor returned with the reusable grocery bags full of leftovers, their shoes, keys, and Abigail's purse. "Ready, Babbi?" they asked.

"Yeah," Abigail said. She gave her mother a look. How it read on her face, she had no idea, but it was meant to be something admonishing.

"Do you need to use the bathroom before we go?" Jor asked.

Mom winked Abigail's way, then swept over to Jordan to give them a hug.

"I'm good." Turning back towards the interior of the cozy rancher, Abigail yelled from the foyer in the general direction of the kitchen where Dad was still sitting at the table, reading a recent newspaper. "Love you Dad! Bye!"

"Drive safe!" he said back.

That'd really been all it had taken to plant the whole concept of pregnancy in this particular timeline in Abigail's mind. She hadn't thought of it much recently. In the early days of her and Jor's relationship, it had been a frequent thought, the baby bug feverish and strong. Early conversations just before and after they moved in together consisted of daydreaming about baby names and looking at adorable toys in various stores. One of their favorites was a non-powered toy store, the classic toys kids would have played within an era before technology took over as the preferred babysitter of parents everywhere. It featured puzzle toys, things that whirred and whizzed with a little motion, stuffed animals, dolls and figurines, and incredibly illustrated books. Abigail and Jordan would walk through the store picking up every little thing that caught their eye, talking about how their kids wouldn't grow up in the same trap as the modern American child.

That particular affliction had faded as quickly as it came. Once they'd moved in together, they focused on painting the walls and decorating, and every picture they hung on the walls or took of themselves in their new life together drew them further from the vision of a family, focusing simply on being a new couple.

Those were wonderful days, full of living, new food, the best sex of their young lives, and constant conversation. Recently, there were still lots of moments of living, less new food and now what felt like old favorites, familiar, yet still great sex, and conversations, but more about bills and date plans than their entire future.

Pregnancy felt like a pair of defibrillator paddles in their relationship, something shocking and life-giving. A reorienting purpose. A place to focus their vision as a couple. It felt good, and admittedly, very uncertain. But, what did they lack in the world? Nothing. Nothing except, maybe, a family of their own.

The phlebotomist walked in from the hall and right over to the tray beside Abigail, picking up the rubber strip.

"Right or left arm, dear?" she asked.

Wordlessly, Abigail held out her left. Her eyes were closed now, and she felt faintly nauseous. Breathing sharply, she tried to think of Mom. Of Jor. It barely registered as the band tied around her arm and the wet cotton swab swiped over her vein. What did register was the pinch of the needle.

Abigail suddenly felt like the world existed only in the crook of her arm. She'd never had an issue with blood draws before. But, the world was different now. She was different. She was having a *baby*. Holy shit that was a lot of pressure. Not just in her life, in her elbow, the vein feeling like it might pop. Though it was a span of a breath and over, that breath was like sucking pebbles through a straw, stuttering and wrong.

"All done."

Clamping a hand over the band-aid, Abigail smiled weakly at the unknown woman, then stood. "Any idea how long it'll take for the results?"

"We're going to do our best to rush it for you. Holidays and all. Fortunately for you, not many people have come in here, holidays and all. Hopefully, our lab will get back to you before we close for New Year's Eve tomorrow afternoon. If not, expect to hear back on the second."

"Thank you."

As she followed the arrows back out, through the lobby, and out to the car, Abigail kept her hand over the band-aid. There was a foreboding sense as if she didn't hold tight all of her would pour out through the tiny hole.

Was she lying to herself?

No. She couldn't be. Things were set in motion now and there was no going back. The future was all but settled now.

SHARING

To partake of, experience, or enjoy with others;
to tell thoughts, feelings, experiences.

JORDAN

New Years Eve was the day Abigail and Jordan had been looking forward to all year. Twenty-nineteen had been a proverbial dumpster fire. From all the inexplicable politics that made up Trump's entire presidency to the fire at Notre Dame and in the Amazon rainforest, the death of Toni Morrison (one of Jordan's idols), mass gun violence, rising White nationalism, an increase in anti-LGBTQ+ hate groups, and so on, it was just a year needing to be abandoned to rot. There was no way 2020 could be any worse. The fresh slate was something Jordan was looking forward to despite knowing that the changing of a clock and calendar was truly arbitrary and meant nothing in the grand scheme of things. Still, the symbolism was nice to lean on. They were all about symbolism in this household.

Tonight, they were going to announce to their closest friends and family about the pregnancy. The blood test had come back with a significant level of HCG, indicating Abbi was as far as they could tell without an ultrasound or a heartbeat, pregnant. Jordan's father, Darrel, was at his high culture coffee shop in Chicago, his dream business he was calling "The French imPress." He specialized in perfectly French-pressed coffees and custom drinks. He'd only recently opened it and he was hosting a New Year event, so they planned to phone call him in for the reveal.

Abbi invited her parents Margie and Jim down from Lancaster, PA, promising they could stay overnight in their new home and check out the city the next day. It was a few hour drive for them which Margie had complained loudly about on the phone leading to much eye-rolling from Jordan. This woman would look for any reason to complain.

They'd also invited Josh, of course, as well as Erica and Alex. Erica and Alex were very close friends of theirs. Erica and Abbi had a casual romantic history that even now lingered in the sort of way only polyamorous folks were likely to understand. Their respect for each other ran deep, and though they were affectionate and even went out on dates occasionally, few ever understood the nature of their relationship. Jordan was all in support of it though, even if it defied conventional labels. How couldn't they? Erica was a supportive friend, thoughtful confidant, and overall great fun to hang out with for both of them.

Erica and Alex were the first to arrive early in the day. Alex lofted a giant fruit and veggie platter above his head as he came in, putting it on the counter before bear-hugging Jordan. Jordan always loved his hugs. Erica came in after with a basket full of wine, holding it up like a trophy.

"We are gonna get crazy tonight!" she cheered. "Fuck 2019!"

The four laughed together, though Jordan caught the little flicker across Abigail's face as she realized no more wine for another nine months or so, if not way longer.

Jordan was acutely aware with Erica here now that she might be caught just as off guard by this whole baby development as they had been.

The living room and dining room were immaculately decorated in blue and silver, a festive solstice scene full of icicle lights and snowflakes. Abbi had gone all out with her enthusiasm, tiny snowmen on the counters, an elaborate fake-floral centerpiece on the dining table, and holiday table runners on every surface. A small tree sat in the front window with glittery ornaments, garland, and lights flashing in an upbeat pattern.

"Nice blue balls you've got," Alex joked, tapping one of the ornaments from beneath.

"No blue balls 'cept those in this house," Jordan teased back. "Something you need to get off your chest over there, buddy?"

Erica rolled her eyes affectionately and clapped a hand on Alex's backside. "You are totally a straight man, sometimes, you know. But I do love you."

"Alright, alright. Let's get all the innuendos out of the way before Mom gets here!" Abbi said, a nervous titter in her otherwise boisterous voice.

Jordan said, "Yes, the party pooper of the century, Missus Margie Miller and her lovely Command Sergeant Major Jim will probably be here in about an hour, so we better shoot all the shit and get the fun over quick."

Erica wound her way through the maze of décor to wrap her arms around Abbi and give her an affectionate kiss on the cheek. "You're looking cheerful," she said, indicating Abbi's choice in a red Santa-inspired dress that clashed with all the silver and blue in the space.

"I'm feeling it," Abbi said, giving her a peck back.

They drifted off to the couch for a proper snuggle.

Jordan watched the two women fondly as they sorted various finger foods out on the counter. Being plant-based themselves, Abbi and Jordan had opted for mostly vegetarian snacks, but they also knew Sergeant Jim would burst like an overripe Republican tomato if there wasn't some kind of meat. With this in mind, they'd put on a hot pot of Swedish meatballs and franks.

Josh was the next to arrive, carrying a box full of various roasted seasoned nuts, a cheese ball, and some more wine.

Alex couldn't help himself and rattled off approximately twenty more jokes about balls and nuts before another knock sounded at the door. Abbi bound from the couch like a spring snake erupting from one of those trick can toys.

Already not her typical charismatic self, Abbi was flustered, she answered the door. Jordan shook their head, watching the way their confident, capable wife so quickly lost her composure when her parents arrived.

"M-mom! Dad! It's so good to see you," she said. "I'm so glad you made it!" She opened her arms to receive stiff hugs from both parents, before gesturing them all the way inside. "Come in, please. Welcome to our new house!"

Jim, his white Colonel Sanders mustache bristling as he sniffed, looked around with an expression so unimpressed, Jordan could feel their stomach knot up just as tight as Abbi's heartstrings always did. Margie stood with her hands on her hips, chin lifted to look around at the décor. Her Karen haircut alone made Jordan feel ill.

"Well, you've decorated it nicely enough," Margie said, turning back toward Abbi after a perfunctory glance around the space. "It's a little small though, isn't it? I didn't see any big houses in the neighborhood, really. It's all townhouses. Are you sure you're going to be comfortable here?"

"Yes, Mom. It's three stories, and the place is really comfy. We even have two spare rooms we've not figured out what to do with yet, and a home office, and a guest bed. The master is really nice, and wait 'til you see our shower."

"Well, if you're happy, Abigail," Margie started, but Jordan turned their attention away from the conversation.

It made them feel beyond nauseated to watch any kind of exchange between the two. Abigail's sheer, bottomless desire to impress her mother was all too often a driving force in her decision making. Their eyes flickered to Abbi's belly, and they felt a rush of the anxiety they hadn't acknowledged since finding out they'd been successful.

What if all of this was just about making Margie happy and Abbi regretted having a kid in five years? Jordan dismissed this flight of thought as swiftly as they could, knowing well all it took to sour their mood was thinking about Margie's impact a little too much. Jordan had to accept a while ago that this was the family they were marrying into. With Abbi came the bigots. Really, it was impressive that Abigail was as well adjusted as she was, as open-minded, progressive, and understanding of Jordan's complex feelings around the issue. More impressively, perhaps, was the fact that Jim and Margie still happened to visit at all given their daughter married someone who used they/them pronouns and was unapologetically, visibly queer and Black. But, even that had come with no insignificant amount of turmoil. They must love their daughter, after all.

Jim meandered to the Swedish meatballs and helped himself to a plate full of animal products, giving Jordan a once over.

"How is work?" he asked with clear difficulty.

"It's great," Jordan said, taking the opportunity to push the line a little while Abbi was out of the room. She'd gone off to give her mom a tour. "I got a promotion and started a new initiative at work for queer kids. Oh, and helped our counseling and social work department have more outreach in the community to help our Black and LGBTQ+ pop get fair treatment. Might be sitting on a board for the local gays group here soon."

"That's..." Jim's mustache danced like a caterpillar on his lip, wriggling in discomfort. "Good for you about the promotion."

As he left to sit down on the couch and turned on the TV, Jordan raked a hand through their tight curls and tried to fight off the impending headache with a swig of wine. That wasn't going to help the headache, actually, but it might make the in-laws more tolerable.

"How are you doing, Jor?" Erica asked.

"I'm just fine," they said through their teeth.

"You're about as fine as a baby bird in a rainstorm."

"Apt. So, how are things at the animal shelter?" Jordan asked quickly, changing the topic at the mention of baby anything. They wanted to spill the news, but also wanted to wait for Abigail to be a part of it.

"Oh, it's great. A lot of people came in to adopt right before the holidays. I hope that they'll actually, you know, keep the pets. Sometimes people are terrible about adopting cats and dogs as gifts for their kids, and then when the kids don't take care of them properly..." She spread her fingers in a "It'll be what it'll be" sort of gesture, then moved her hands to her scalp to pull her blonde hair up into a high ponytail. She unlooped a hair tie from her wrist to secure the style, then went on.

"Worst case, they come back to the shelter and I get to play with them again, I guess. I don't mind. We're a no-kill shelter. Though, it does get overwhelming when there's so many animals packed in like lil' sausages."

"Yeah, I bet. Hey, you want some wine?"

"Mmm, yeah."

Alex and Josh were in the living room standing by the window whispering conspiratorially about something, and save for the presence of the Millers, it was a pretty comfortable moment. Erica had a way of calming Jordan down when no one else could. She was kind-hearted and intelligent like Abbi, but Jordan wasn't heart-splitting, breath-stealing in love with her. The separation there allowed Erica to intervene with Jordan's moods in a way that sometimes Abbi only heightened them.

Guilt crept in. The last thing Jordan wanted was for Erica to feel the same shock they had. Erica deserved to be kept in the loop. She was the closest emotionally to Abbi and them, and they could only imagine how sour they'd be if Alex and Erica sprung big news on them at the same time as their parents.

"Hey, Erica... I want to tell you something, but you can't tell Abs I told you, alright?"

Erica's gaze zoned in on Jordan so fast, her ponytail whipped her in the side of the face. She winced but regained her composure with an admirable swiftness. "Yes?"

It was then that Abbi came back downstairs with Margie in tow, announcing by the rough clearing of her throat that she was ready.

"Oh boy," Jordan murmured.

"Later?" Erica said.

"Nope. It's too late."

Erica looked momentarily confused, but Jordan knew it'd all click in a second.

"Everyone," Abigail was saying loudly, and Jordan felt the breath leave their body like the very spirit was draining from them. "Jor and I have something we'd like to share with you!"

Alex and Josh stopped whispering to turn back toward the living room. Erica came out of the kitchen to stand next to the table, her fingers lightly resting on one of the shimmery winter-themed placemats. Jordan picked up the remote from the arm of the couch and quickly flicked the TV off, much to the dismay of Jim who was watching Fox News. Margie crossed her arms as Jordan navigated from the couch to wrap their own around Abbi.

Abbi coughed, scraping at the anxiety Jordan knew was trapped like a jar of bees. Jordan could feel her nerves vibrating as her body gently shook. They tightened their hold a little, protective.

With no more fanfare, Abigail announced, "Jor and I are having a baby."

Margie's knees buckled, and she dropped like a Hollywood actress on camera, a hand rising to clutch not just her metaphorical, but her literal pearls. She started sobbing immediately.

The rest of the room was mute. In the distance, a car alarm went off. Abigail looked around, waiting for someone to say something.

It was Josh who spoke up first.

"Oh shit," he said as it hit. "Woah. It. WOW, y'all. Congratulations! Does this mean I'm sorta like an Uncle now? Is that weird?"

"Adopting?" came the question from Jim before anyone else could say anything. His voice was flat and unaffected.

"No, I'm carrying." Abbi puffed herself up like a bull on the range, shoulders squaring as she stepped away from Jordan to help her mother back to her feet.

Jordan knew the next thing said was going to spoil it all. They were right.

Tearful, Margie looked up and said, "So the baby will be...?"

"Be what, Margie?" Jordan snapped.

They knew very well what likely existed in that question. *So the baby will be White? Biologically my grandchild?*

Not of this inferior person's bloodline with their family history of medical problems and their dark skin? Jordan felt hot with a ripple of rage that rose from their toes to scalp.

Margie managed to shut her mouth. For that, Jordan was grateful. Better to only think there was some racist connotation there than have it confirmed again.

"Josh was our donor!" Abigail said, excitement returning to her voice. Or was it anxiety? For once, Jordan had trouble telling.

Margie swiveled on Josh, staring the lanky Black man down. "Well." she said, "The baby will... Look a bit like Jordan then."

Jordan imagined Abigail knew the implications of what Margie was saying, but she said only, "Yeah! They are built so similarly and both have gorgeous jawlines."

Sparing a glance at Erica, Jordan saw she was still as a photo, staring blankly not at Abigail, but at Alex like she needed a lifeline. Alex looked back with an expression of bewilderment, eyebrows shot up towards his mousy brown hairline.

"Shall we celebrate?" Abigail asked.

"Yes. Let me pour lots of wine for everyone." Jordan turned back to the kitchen where they selected one of the now five available wines.

"Not for little miss Abigail, though!" Margie cried, taking a stumbling step after Jordan.

Once again through their teeth, Jordan said, "Of course."

Jordan was a little irritated that Abbi had forgotten to call Darrel for the announcement, so they went out on the back porch to video chat him while everyone else began making plates of food. In the end, it was better this way. Darrel was all the support and cheer that Margie and Jim hadn't been. None of the tension. His response lifted Jordan's spirits once again. He hoisted a mug of coffee to the two of them, steam billowing on the small screen. All smiles. Laughter. What a parent-child relationship should be.

"To my baby and their future baby, and of course my baby-in-law," he said with a wink. "You two are going to be great. Teach that little one to burn the world down, alright?"

Jordan felt the familiar pang of grief as yet another important event went by that their mother wouldn't get to see—taken still young and eternally beautiful by a chronic disease. This, too, they swallowed down for Abbi's sake.

The next few hours went about as expected. Everyone save Abbi drank, some to excess, while the New Years Special on NBC with Carson Daly blared in the background. Abi sat with her mother talking about baby plans, and Jim ate a solid majority of the meatballs and franks, patting his belly and passing out on the couch around 10:30. Alex and Josh began a card game at the table, both buzzed men talking emphatically about the best combos.

Erica swooped in on Jordan at the first possible chance they had to be alone.

"What the fuck?" she said, grabbing Jordan by the upper arm.

"I wanted to tell you," Jordan said.

"Are you sure this is what the two of you wanted?" Erica asked, ignoring the statement.

"Abs kinda sprung it on me before Christmas, and you know how she gets when she's enthusiastic. You can't help but go along with her schemes."

"Scheme alright. And no, you can't help but go along with her schemes. She didn't tell me about this at all."

"Me either until the night we went through with it. Apparently, she d talked to Josh about it, and Margie was the one that planted the idea in her head in the first place." Jordan felt a little nauseous stating it aloud, the wine in their belly seeming to ferment with every word and movement.

"Of course she did. Jor, I... I don't know what to say. But, I will do my best to be happy for you. That is if you're happy."

Jordan chewed their lip for a moment, a nervous tick of theirs. "I..." They looked over at Erica's intense stare, her amber eyes alive with concern. "Yes. I am happy. I don't like Margie's involvement in it at all, and I hope Abbi is doing this for the right reasons, you know? I do feel like maybe I shouldn't have gone along with it so quickly, but at the same time I didn't expect her to get knocked up the first time I shoved a turkey baster in her."

"Oh my God, you used a turkey baster?" That broke Erica's tension, and she laughed until she had to wipe her eyes. "Sometimes y'all are so stereotypical I can't stand it. But, hey, props for doing it on the cheap."

After a good sob in Abbi's arms, doting on how good of a mother she'd make and how happy she was for her and Jordan, Margie wandered into the kitchen to Jordan. Erica slipped off to go talk with Abigail, leaving the mother-in-law and her child-in-law alone. Still tearful, Margie lifted her arms up to Jordan. The sick feeling came back triple time, but Jordan accepted the hug.

"I'm glad the two of you could figure your way around this... Hiccup," Margie said.

"Hiccup?" Jordan asked, already dreading the answer.

"Yes, since you couldn't get her pregnant."

Jordan's voice snapped across the room like a crackle of lightning, jolting anyone along the way. "I mean, I was the one who got her pregnant."

Margie interrupted with a wave of her hand. "Oh, I don't need the details. You know what I mean."

Jordan did, unfortunately, but that didn't make it feel any better. "I'm glad Abbi is happy. That's all," Jordan said instead of telling this old hag to go suck something sour.

As the ball dropped at midnight, Jordan mustered up all the will they contained, and lifted a glass of wine toward the ceiling. Around them, Erica, Josh, and Alex lifted their glasses, too. Abbi had sparkling cider, as did Margie, and Jim had roused himself with another beer brought in from the car.

It was Jordan who cleared their throat this time. "To 2020. To a future we never imagined. To a year a helluva lot better than 2019. To the best friends in the world. To my in-laws for driving so far out this way to see our new place. To the streets of Hampden we call home. And to my beautiful wife and our future child."

There was a little cheer from their friends, though slight tension still curled like a vine around Jordan's throat. They looked down at Abbi, forced a smile, and once again assured themselves that as long as she was happy, everything was okay.

PERSPECTIVE

The capacity to view things in their truth or relative importance; a mental view.

Erica

Packages from Margie started arriving at their doorstep as early as the next week, despite both Abbi and Jor protesting and telling her not to buy things yet.

Erica knew this because of the almost hilariously shocked phone call from Abbi where she'd said something along the lines of, "How can she be buying stuff this early? We don't even know 100% for sure that I'm pregnant! I haven't even had the damn ultrasound yet!"

As Alex dropped Erica off at Abbi and Jor's front door, a UPS truck was pulling up just a house down. A man in the classic brown uniform hopped out, delivered a package to the neighbor, then went back to the truck to grab something else. Once Erica kissed Alex goodbye, she stood back and watched as Alex peeled away around the big truck at the same time as the man delivered yet another large box to the front steps of the Robins' place.

With a laugh, Erica went to the front door and picked up the bulky box, struggling to hold it while she prodded the doorbell with an outstretched finger.

It was Jor who answered, casually dressed in shorts, a sports bra, and a robe. They looked like a boxer about to waltz out into the ring.

"Did you...?"

Erica quickly shook her head. "Wasn't me. Promise. It just got here at the same time as I did."

Abbi arrived behind Jordan, peeking around them to see Erica and the box. She was dressed for their brunch date in a daisy print white dress, her coppery hair braided and coiled in a thick bun on top of her head. Erica always thought Abbi's face was particularly striking framed in a few strands of hair.

Spotting the box, however, Abbi groaned, her head tipping back in a caricature of horror.

"Moms will be moms?" Abbi and Jordan said simultaneously.

Erica giggled. These two were always in sync.

"Haven't lost our lesbian mind-meld, I guess," Abbi said with a grin, nuzzling into Jordan's chest. When she pulled away, she took the box from Erica and handed it off to Jordan. "We'll be back later!"

Grabbing her keys from their hook and putting on a coat, Abbi followed Erica back outside into the bracing January morning. It was too damn cold, but the sky was clear and bright, the pale blue barely marked with white clouds.

Leaning into Erica, Abbi wrapped an arm around her. "You must be freezing," she said.

Agreeing, Erica gave a quick nod. "Yes, so can we get in the car quick?"

They bolted down the street to where Abbi's car was parallel parked, practically leaping in at the first opportunity. Abbi cranked the engine and set the heater to max hot, then looked across the seat toward her partner.

"Erica, I'm sorry," she said. It was their first time alone at all since New Years. Since the announcement. "I didn't consider your feelings. How you might want to know about this before we told anyone else."

Fiddling with her own hair, Erica pulled her lips in over her teeth, biting down a little. She hadn't expected this much directness from Abbi so quickly on their date. Abbi was not one to be very forthcoming at times, especially not when it came to feelings, stressors, or 'Big Plans'. This had perhaps been 'The Biggest Plan Yet', so Erica was both unsurprised she'd not been kept in the loop, and also understanding. Abbi liked flashy reveals sometimes. Last-minute surprises. And, when she tended to have "Aha!" moments, they were rife with wide eyes, open mouths, and expressions of absolute embarrassment. Abbi never wanted to be seen as anything other than perfect.

"Abbi," Erica said, leaning back against the car's seat. She wound her ponytail around her knuckles, not wanting the date to be nothing but unpacking Abbi's lack of awareness. It'd been a while since they'd had a solo date. Work had seemed so busy lately.

"I know," Abbi said, interrupting Erica from her wandering thoughts. "I talked to Josh first, then Jory, then no one else until we told everyone. In hindsight, I probably should have told you before we attempted to knock me up... Well, and succeeded." She gave what sounded like a nervous tittering laugh, then looked down at her lap. "I want you to know I value you as a partner. I love you. And you're way more important to me than I realize this probably caused you to feel."

With a sigh, Erica reached across and touched Abbi's hand, grateful for her vulnerability, and for her car's heat.

"It's... Thank you," Erica said. "I would have liked to know, before, yes. But, it's happened and we can't go back in time now, can we?"

With a little shake of her head, Abbi dragged her gaze up to meet Erica's. She looked different, somehow, like being pregnant matured her just a touch more. Looking at Abbi when she was so emotionally open always did Erica in. She could completely understand why Jory often had the same experience. Why it was so easy to give into Abbi, even when she made choices that led to them hurting?

This was her greatest flaw, for sure. Her lack of overall appreciation for how others were impacted by her actions. Sometimes, Abbi seemed to be in her own little world, and maybe that was a product of her upbringing. Of her privilege. The way Margie doted on her and always made sure she got her way—at least to a point.

"We can talk more about it later," Erica said, finally drawing her eyes away from Abbi. "I'm cold and hungry, and I am ready to eat some very fluffy, very warm pancakes."

With that, Abbi drove. They turned on some Mary Lambert in the car and sang along together, both slightly off-key. Jory was the most musically gifted among them, by far. Funnily enough, Erica and Abbi met in middle school chorus class. They weren't that great then, either. Abbi never could read the sheet music, and Erica was just bored with it. But, singing pretend karaoke on their boomboxes at sleepovers? Wonderful. Blasting music in the car while they cruised and pretended to be rock stars? All the better.

Leaving Hampden, they drove into Towson to grab their brunch at a generic breakfast haunt, a diner they'd loved for what seemed like ages. The gleaming silvery seats and the neon décor always evoked a sense of being young again, alive at a time where there were no worries.

They sat down and ordered: a fruit cup, eggs, and a half-stack of pancakes for Abbi; a full-stack for Erica with a side of bacon and home fries.

"Are you trying to eat any particular way now that you're *reasonably* certain you're pregnant?" Erica asked, a glint of amusement in her eyes as she recalled the packages from Margie and the resulting conversations.

"Yeah. It's inspired me to try some non-plant-based, pure high protein sources like eggs and occasionally really high-quality organic meat. I'll probably do some bone broths, too; I want this baby to be healthier than I am, you know?" She patted her tummy gently.

"Whatever works for you and the baby, I'm glad to support. When does morning sickness and stuff start?"

"Not quite yet, but any day now if it's going to happen."

Abbi smiled as the waiter brought her cup of apple juice and set a coffee down in front of Erica. Both of them sipped their drinks, looking over the rims at each other for a moment.

There had always been an ease between Erica and Abbi, spanning as far back as they could remember. It was hard to actually pinpoint when their romantic relationship had begun because they'd always seemed so close. They didn't have a formal anniversary or anything like that, and it didn't really matter to them. Once, they'd talked about whether or not their relationship really needed labels, but that hadn't been something either of them particularly cared about. Instead, they'd just settled on "partners," though by most cishet normative standards, they weren't in a relationship at all. They had no intentions of getting married, living together, or even having sex except perhaps once a year or so, usually when they took a mutual weekend getaway to Rehoboth Beach or drove out into the Adirondacks for some air and fresh perspective.

Erica reached across and put her hand on top of Abbi's. "I'm happy for you and Jory. You two will make genuinely good parents. I hope we'll still be able to find time for each other once the baby comes, and that you'll let me dote on them and teach them swear words."

With mirthful laughter, Abbi nodded. "Of course. I need a corrupting force to balance out my Mother."

At the mention of Margie, Erica chewed her lower lip, debating. Was it worth bringing up how she worried Abbi rushed this decision to make her mom happy? That she worried Jor had given in to Abbi's desires as they always did, no matter their own feelings? Erica was often the one that called Abbi out, but she was already pregnant. What could be done now?

With as much tact as she could summon, she gave Abbi's hand a squeeze and said, "I hope you and Jor can really raise this child the way *you* want to, without much outside influence. If your mother had her way, you'd be raising this kid in the evangelical church and probably feeding them Captain Crunch every morning like it was a balanced breakfast because it had 'fruit berries' in it."

Giggles escaped from between Abbi's closed lips, her cheeks puffing up a little. "What an image," she said. "But, you're right. Sometimes I'm a tempted to listen to Mom's suggestions so she doesn't sulk, but I think when it comes to this baby, my own Momma Bear spirit is going to come out on top."

"I hope you're right," Erica said, thumb brushing over Abbi's knuckles.

In all of Erica's memories of being around Margie growing up, that woman had always been a swaying force to Abbi. "You should take art instead of shop. Shop isn't going to be that useful for your future," or "That dress makes you look pudgy. Wear this one." It was a lot of the classic White mom stuff. With that also came the White mom guilt tactics when Abbi pushed back or disagreed with something. "You must think I'm a terrible mother!" and "All I want is what's best for you! I'm sorry!"

It was exhausting to witness. Erica's upbringing with a single mother had been somehow easier. Her mom was pretty progressive. She got them roped into lots of volunteer projects, especially with animals and the homeless. And, she'd always supported Erica in doing whatever she wanted to do.

That included supporting Erica's polyamorous lifestyle, which had a far wider web than Abbi's. Erica was with Abbi, Alex, and a couple named Trish and Ron, who she'd met around the same time that Abbi and Jordan got together.

On the complete opposite side of the spectrum, Abbi's mother had been confused when Abbi started dating Jordan. She'd known that Abbi and Erica were in some kind of relationship. When Jordan came along and met the family, there had apparently been a whole to do afterward about how it was sinful to have more than one relationship—even though the Bible had many "non-traditional" relationships, including polygamous ones. When Abbi stormed out midway through the conversation, Margie had actually called Erica for support.

After Erica confirmed that her and Abbi were still in a relationship, that nothing had changed, that she was okay with it, and reminded Margie gently that she had a husband herself. That seemed to calm Margie a little. Margie liked Erica, after all.

It had always been easier for Margie to accept people who were "different" when they weren't directly in her family.

After meeting Jordan for the first time though and finding out the "secret," as Margie called it, she reached out to Erica with something even more direct and more problematic.

"I'm worried about Abbi's future if she stays with Jordan," Margie said.

"Why? They're lovely, have a great job, and they make Abbi insanely happy."

"But, she's colored," Margie said, her voice low, almost conspiratorial. But, there was fear there, too.

Erica had felt deflated in that moment, scared for what might happen if Margie said such a thing to her daughter. Biting back the initial retorts she wanted to fire at the woman, she instead said, "First of all, Jordan is nonbinary.

Second, what does them being Black have to do with literally anything?"

"I'm..." There was a pause as if Margie were looking around, then she came back. "I'm worried about Dad and Jack coming down hard on Abbi for being in an interracial relationship. You know how they feel about colored people."

Unfortunately, Erica did. She'd been around the Miller family enough to know that Jack and Jim Miller were about as bigoted as they came. For all Abbi loved her mother, she didn't interact with her father unless she had to. Her brother, Jack, she avoided at all costs. He wasn't welcome to family gatherings that took place on Abbi's own turf. It was definitely true that there was likely to be some conflict if ever Jack met Jor.

"I do, but... That should never stop Abbi from being with someone she wants to be with. Love is love, Margie."

"I do wish you'd call me Mom," she said, quickly.

When you start acting like everyone's mom and not just the people who do things your way, I will, Erica thought, but said instead, "Love is love."

"I know, I know. I just..." There was a long sigh, the kind that trembles as it tapers out. "I just worry about my girl. She's done so well for herself in life, despite everything that her father thought she couldn't do. I'm so proud of her. I don't want to see her dreams destroyed because America isn't ready for mixed relationships."

If looking around Baltimore was any indication, that definitely wasn't true—more like racist families weren't ready for mixed relationships.

Carried away from the date with all the memories, it took the waiter sitting down their plates full of food to remember she was on the date with Abbi.

"Abbi, what made you decide it was time to get pregnant?"

There was a look that passed over Abbi's face, one Erica interpreted as conflicted. Was she trying to come up with a good story? They'd been in each other's lives plenty long enough to know that whatever Abbi was about to say would be a half truth, something plausible but not entirely the full story.

"Well, Mom brought it up at Thanksgiving and I'd been thinking about it for a while before that anyway, so..."

Erica shook her head, spearing a bite of homefry. "No you haven't. I *know* I'd have heard about it before the surprise announcement if that were the case. Was this another of your fly-by-your-ass decisions?"

Looking thoroughly scolded, Abbi poked at her fruit. "I... Maybe."

Erica sighed, leaning forward, propping her elbow on the table, and settling her chin onto a fist. "So, Margie brought it up at Thanksgiving and you...?"

"I started thinking of it a lot more then. I mean, to be totally fair, Jory and I talked about it a lot in the beginning. But, once Mom brought it up, it was like I got her blessing to maybe go forward with having a baby with Jory, and then it just... It infected me again, the whole idea."

Studying Abbi's face as she spoke, Erica knew now she was getting into the realm of truth. "Figures. So now that it's actually happening, how do you feel?"

"Scared, I guess. Wondering if I am going to be a good mother. If I'll have time for all the other people I love, like you. Wondering if I'll ever get to write my books. Trying to figure out if I am pregnant because it's what I really want or if I'm..."

She stopped speaking suddenly, her throat tightening as she swallowed. Erica ripped a piece of bacon in half, waiting. When Abbi didn't speak after she ate both halves, she waved a hand in front of her face.

"Earth to Abbi. You're burying something, aren't you?"

"Yeah," she said. Picking up her juice, she took a long gulp, then cupped it in her fingers. She couldn't seem to look at Erica.

"What if, and I literally loathe this very idea, what if I'm covering up for something with the idea of a baby? An idea I'm now very much decided in, clearly."

Erica did her best not to smirk. "What would you be covering up for?"

"That's the part that really bothers me. I don't know."

"Are things good with Jordan?"

Abigail's hold on her fork slipped and it plummeted right into her orange juice glass. "What!? Of course they are. Why do you ask?"

Erica took another bite, chewing slowly, trying to give Abbi enough space to puzzle through it all. She could be thick sometimes. So full of ideas and inspiration, compassion, and kindness, but also self-blindness, like the light to her inner world was turned out. Or at least, that was how it appeared from the outside. Erica wasn't Abbi after all. She couldn't actually see inside her partner's head, much as she'd like to. But, when the answer seemed so obvious, she wondered why Abbi couldn't just blurt it out.

Fishing her fork back out, Abbi wiped it on a napkin looking rather affronted. "Of course they're good. I don't know if we've ever been happier than we are now to have this new... New purpose? I almost said project, but a kid isn't a project and Jory would probably glare me to death if they heard me say that." Abandoning her food, she wrung her hands, fingers gliding over their twins.

"Do you not feel unified anymore?"

"No, I definitely think we do. Things have been good. Lots of dates. Lots of intimacy. It's like we've got it all... Everything except children, right?" She paused, staring down at her plate of pancakes, and with what looked like a summoning of courage, finally sliced in and took a bite.

"Right... Everything but children," Erica said.

"And well, we've done everything else. Maybe a little outta order. Met. Dated. Moved in together. Got engaged. Got married. Cute home. Is there anything left to do but have kids?"

The imprint of societal expectations in this moment was so obvious it might as well have been stamped across Abbi's forehead. Erica frowned, distracting herself with her bacon. The two of them had been 'Fuck Society' Crusaders for as long as she could remember, and seeing how easily Abbi could get swept back into it just by Margie bringing the topic up was not only painful, it was embarrassing. For Erica who was actively avoiding society's rules with her non-legal husband, yard full of progressive social justice signs. and multiple relationships all with very different definitions of intimacy, there were no kids on the radar. And she certainly felt complete.

"Well, only you can determine that, I guess," Erica said. She reached across to gently pat Abbi's hand. "No matter what, I've got your back, but seriously, please don't leave me out of any big thoughts or major decisions in the future? I at least want to follow along with your thinking. Know where you're at."

Abbi nodded. "Yeah. Again, I'm sorry. Got wrapped up in my own head and I guess went a little too far with the concept of surprise. You shouldn't have found out at the same time as everyone else."

"Thank you. I forgive you," Erica said, though she couldn't help but feel a distant pang of something over the fact Jor had thought to tell her first. "Now... Tell me all about your plans for the baby's room, and have you narrowed down names?"

From Erica's perspective, even though Abbi had a shield around her feelings that was as dense as a heavy metal sometimes, she was going to make a good mother. Anywhere she might lack, Jordan was going to fill things in perfectly. Erica was genuinely happy for them. The only nagging worry that lingered was Margie's unsolicited opinions looming over the Robins' relationship and how that may affect their child. She just had to hold out hope that Abbi and Jor were indeed as strong together as Abbi declared them to be.

ANTICIPATION

The act of looking forward; a prior action that takes into account some future action.

Abigail

Abigail lay flat on the cold table, wrapping her arms around herself. The hospital gown she'd been told to wear was open in the front, exposing her bare, round belly. Her stomach showed above her breasts from her point of view, not because she was visibly pregnant but because that was just how her body was shaped. It had been that way for as long as she could remember—at least as long as she'd been getting her periods. Where most girls got breasts and body hair, she got it all, plus a little extra. The teasing had, she supposed, only served to further pad the extra until she was a soft as a pillow putting on a brave face for the world.

Jordan sat reading one of the provided pamphlets in their examination room. This one featured cute illustrations of fruit, showing the timeline of pregnancy from conception to birth. Jor hummed an old song, something by Little Richard, Abbi thought. Dragging her eyes away from her stomach, she instead traced the lines on the drop tile ceilings. Waiting felt excruciating, a small slice of eternity.

Around the time Abbi thought she'd counted exactly how many squares were on the ceiling (those made of 1 tile, 4 tiles, 9 tiles, etc), Dr. Diaz stepped in.

"Afternoon, Robinses," she said, walking over to the counter to put on gloves and peek over the clipboard left of her. "So, I understand you're about 10 weeks along and this is your first major checkup. I'm glad to work with you."

The doc offered both Jor and Abigail a smile. "Do you know what to expect at the first appointment like this?"

Abigail nodded. "I've done some research," she said.

"Some," Jordan said.

Dr. Diaz seemed to understand the downplay and rather than explaining everything in detail, she said, "Alright, so I understand you just want to do a fetal heartbeat at this point, not an early ultrasound. That's totally fine. Once we've done the quick physical, gotten the heartbeat, and talked over any concerns, I'll get you over to the lab side for some samples."

"One question though. Can you remind me what all the bloodwork is for?" She had an uneasy feeling from the first blood draw, that feeling of the world beginning to zoom in on one minuscule prick of light.

"We check for Rh factor, anemia, immunity to rubella, Hep B, and STIs. We also do a complete blood count, TB check, and... Do you have any history in your family of diabetes?"

"No."

"We do have some more pamphlets on the bloodwork if you're curious," Dr. Diaz said, looking more at Jor than Abigail.

Abigail was silent as Dr. Diaz did all the routine poking and prodding of a typical doctor's visit, making notes on a chart. "Your blood pressure was a little high when the nurse took it," she said. "Is that normal?"

"No. Just nervous."

When Diaz seemed satisfied, she stepped back from Abigail and went over to the doppler machine hooked up to a cart.

The doppler machine came to life with faint mechanical whirrings and Dr. Diaz put the rounded end of the machine's rod against Abigail's exposed belly.

There was no sound—at least, no heartbeat.

Jor sat up straight, leaning in. Their eyes flicked between Abigail and Dr. Diaz, brow knit.

"Ah, just give me a moment. I might need to try a few angles."

The doctor pressed the doppler harder against Abigail, plastic cutting into her like a blunt blade. She winced, biting her lower lip. It hurt. The pressure. She closed her eyes tight, face scrunched and desperate to hear her child's heartbeat. Instead, she heard Jordan swallow, gulping what she expected was their own nerves. Dr. Diaz cleared her throat with a little grunt.

Wanting to curl inside herself, Abigail felt the cluster of nerves she'd brought with her into the appointment growing only tighter. They tangled until they were so constricting, she couldn't feel anything else anymore. The room was hot now, a furnace she was going to burn alive in. Her and Jory, putting on a ruse of pregnancy, all the positive tests somehow tricks. The greatest prank of them all.

Thud-thud-thud-thud. At first, a dull sound. Then, Dr. Diaz said, "Got it!" and it grew clearer. The doppler was prodding somewhere under one of Abigail's belly rolls.

To her credit, Dr. Diaz said nothing of Abigail's weight. Instead, she said, "There it is! Sounds like a typical heartbeat."

"Why's it so fast?" Jor asked.

"A fetal heartbeat is usually almost twice what the average adults is. Around 110 to 160. Your baby is at 132 right now."

Abigail felt like she might sob. That confirmation after a moment of such dreadful anticipation, thinking for even a moment that she might not actually be pregnant or a miscarriage had happened. It was a sort of relief she never knew she could have needed before. Grinning at Jor, a few tears eeked their way out from Abigail's reopened eyes. Jor was crying, too. Dr. Diaz let them listen a few more moments, allowing their new life to be confirmed in the span of a few beats.

"So, any questions for me before we get you off to the lab?"

Sitting up, Abigail clutched the hospital gown together. "Well, I've been reading a lot on what to eat and take for supplements and such, but do you have any sage advice?"

"Mmm, listen to your body. Eat what you can, especially if you're nauseous, but go for whole foods as much as possible. Stay hydrated, and of course no caffeine and alcohol. We recommend none of either."

"All the booze for me!" Jordan said.

"Uh huh," Abbi said, sticking her tongue out. "I know weight loss is probably recommended."

Dr. Diaz picked up the clipboard again, looking over it rather than directly at Abigail. "I am a little worried about gestational diabetes, but we can do an early check for that, too. You've had no major health issues in the past, correct?"

"Nope. Couple of broken bones when I was a kid, flu a few times, that kind of thing."

"You shouldn't be too worried then, but we'll run what we can to be safe."

Even though she'd been the one to bring it up, the talk of her body was making Abbi feel like she was in middle school again. She was grateful when Dr. Diaz moved the topic away.

"Any other questions?"

"Yeah," Jor said. "Any advice on how to best support Momma?"

"Happy Mom, happy baby, at least that's the way I see it. So, do whatever makes Mom relaxed and content."

"Lots of snuggles, books, and foot rubs. Got it." Jor winked at Abigail, which she almost missed as she dove for her pile of clothes, wanting nothing more than to cover up again.

"When you're done, just follow the blue arrows in the hall that say lab."

Once Dr. Diaz exited, Jor said, "You okay? You look... Mad."

"Just worried about my weight and the baby. I've read how a lot of people who are 'obese' can't get pregnant. I got lucky, I guess, but like, I don't want to mess it up."

Jor frowned, and Abigail didn't need to be inside their head to know what they were thinking.

"Babbi, what's important is you're pregnant now. You're healthy. You're beautiful. Your weight has little to do with your overall well-being. You've had flawless bloodwork and physicals—"

"My whole life, I know." She sighed, shoving a leg into her pants. "Let's get the other tests done. I'm ready for a foot rub."

Peeing in a cup was simple. Always had been. Bloodwork used to be simple, but now as the phlebotomist approached Abigail's left side, it might as well have been a charging bull. She shrank into herself, fear blossoming outward from her chest and crawling down her arms. Something was wrong. She could feel it in her core, something wanting to be wrenched up and out of her. Something toxic. Threatening. Whatever it was, it felt dangerous.

The needle pierced her vein, digging deep within her to find out if she was healthy. If the baby was healthy. The needle pierced through an invisible barrier, and something in her snapped. Where before had been breath was now holding. Where once she'd been as casual about this sort of visit as an afternoon tea, there was now bracing and resistance. Abigail felt the pressure building again, an internal volcanic eruption on the verge of going over.

Abigail peeled open her damp eyes. Sought out Jory's gaze. Opened her mouth to speak. Instead of words, out came breakfast. Jor startled, said something, but Abigail couldn't hear. She heard only static as her view of the world took on the look of a black-rimmed vignette. The circle closed until all she could see was Jor's panicked face. Then, she was gone.

"Can you hear me, babe? Abbi?"

Sometimes when Abigail stood alone in her classroom after all the kids were gone for the day, she'd turn off the flourescent overhead lights. The difference it made was incredible. The room buzzed with electrical currents, a constant background sound. When she flipped the switch, it was completely silent. The air felt empty. Occasionally, she could hear a vehicle in the distance or another teacher down the hall, little sounds normally drowned out by the constant hum. It was like that now, only in reverse. There had been nothing. Then, there was Jordan.

More sounds thrummed all around, hard to make out. Phones ringing. Lightbulbs. Machines. A hushed conversation. Jordan. Jordan. She anchored onto that one.

"Abbi?"

Glancing down, Abigail saw the vomit. Glancing up, she saw Jordan looking more stoic than ever.

"Are you okay?"

Her mouth tasted sour. "Water?"

Already on it, one of the nurses handed Jordan a cup to give to Abigail. She chugged it, flushed with embarrassment and the acrid taste of her own bile.

They didn't have any other clothes for Abigail to change into. Only the medical smocks. After she was assured it was safe to try and stand up and wash up in the bathroom, they offered her a plain white garment to cover up her shame on the way out of the office.

"What happened?" Jor asked once they were in the bathroom.

"I dunno. Everything just went black. My arm felt like it was going to explode."

"So you decided to instead, eh?"

Abigail smirked in spite of everything. At least she could always count on Jordan maintaining a sense of humor.

NESTING

*In pregnancy, a natural instinct, and intense
drive to prepare the baby's environment
channeled into cleaning, organizing, birth
plans, and/or limiting social gatherings.*

Abigail

Aside from the doctor's visit, life was just normal life for
a bit. The beginning of 2020 was not what they'd hoped
for, what with the devastating wildfires in Australia. But,
the fact that Prince Harry and Meghan Markle essentially
dropped out of the royal family was quite the anarchist
twist Jordan lived for. Abbi and Jordan celebrated at
foraged. with yet another wonderful meal, Abbi playing
around with the carved wooden mushrooms on the table
and chittering away wondering if their child would like
plants and if they could build a moss wall and plant an herb
garden on the porch and...

As usual, Jordan had to remind her to take things one
step at a time.

Often, Jor found Abigail pacing the hallway outside what would soon be the "nursery." Typically, the scene involved her hair pulled up in a fraying bun, Abigail chewing frantically at the end of a pencil with a blank clipboard tucked under an arm.

"What?" Abigail would say when she spotted Jor. What followed was usually, "Mom is making me nervous!" or "What if the baby is born and we haven't even decorated?" or "What if we run out of time!?"

Always, Jor's reply would be a laugh, a hug, then, "We don't have to take on the parenting thing all in a day. We'll figure it out. How about you..." Grade some papers. Write a poem. Eat a snack. Anything to get her mind off worrying.

They didn't hit up the local brewery just off the Avenue quite as much now that Abbi couldn't drink, but they did spend perhaps even more moments at Atomic Books, begging the owner to order all the latest pregnancy titles. Abbi was particularly excited about one Feminist take on pregnancy called Like a Mother by Angela Garbes. It was sad not to be able to routinely attend the parties in the bar at the back of the bookstore given they usually went to drink, but to counteract that, Jordan put a great deal of effort into experimenting with virgin mixed drinks so Abbi could still enjoy herself on their typical Friday evening date nights.

Teaching was taxing Abbi more than usual now that she was pregnant. She was more cautious than usual and didn't want to stress, but stressing about stress made her even more stressed. Jordan tried to convince her to take it just one day at a time, but she never was good at that. After work, she'd clean or fret about the nursery, and on weekends, she'd go on nesting binges, then nap all day.

Jordan did their damnedest to keep things interesting and lighthearted for Abbi. One day while Abbi was at work, they put googly eyes on everything in the fridge so that Abbi nearly peed herself laughing when she got home. Another, they printed a dragon face and taped it over the top of the automatic aromatherapy machine in the living room so every now and then the dragon spit steam. They knew they couldn't do the same startling pranks as before such as putting a cardboard monster in the shower, or spraying whipped cream on Abbi's forehead and hands while she slept, which made for a fun time contemplating new things to do.

Although barely pregnant by anyone's standards, not even far enough to get a good ultrasound image, and barely a heartbeat, Abigail agreed to go preview baby supplies at the store with Mom on a weekend. Her mother was so over the moon now that she'd settled into the news a little more, and they'd agreed to meet up halfway, just around an hour drive for each of them.

"We can just look at the basics," she'd insisted.

Margie pulled Abigail by the sleeve down one of the aisles at Target, cooing at all of the little designs printed on everything from burp cloths and blankies to diapers and onesies. Much like Abigail touched the spine of every book at Atomic, Margie fingered every single shining package, every bit of soft cloth. It was amusing seeing how much her and her mother were alike sometimes. And also terrifying.

What if she was like her mom when she was a mother? Always hovering a little too close. Always offering an opinion when it wasn't necessary. Trying to protect her child from the world through a limited lens of experience. That part was less likely to be the case, but that didn't stop her from panicking a little.

"Oh darling," her mother said, turning to look at her. "This is all so cute. How are you going to decide what to go with?"

Without hesitating, Abbi said, "We really want to go with bumble bees."

"Oh!" Margie sounded a little surprised, her expression perplexed. "Why bees?"

"It's just what Jordan and I agreed on. And it's gender neutral." Abigail really didn't feel like getting into the whole story, mainly because of a comment Jory had made before she'd left.

"Please don't tell your mom the stripes story. I don't think she'd really appreciate it. It... Highlights our differences." Jor had looked far away when they'd said it, almost as if a little disappointed or upset. Abigail left right after though, already running late for the rendezvous with Mom, so she puzzled over the comment in her head instead and respected Jor's wishes.

Apparently Mom was fine with that because she immediately started rummaging shelves for bee things.

"There *are* some cute patterned beehive things and lots of chubby cherub bees, so, I suppose there will be plenty of options, though we might not find much here," Margie said, turning down another row of things to look at. "But, of course, your father and I can order anything you'd like from a registry if you put one together."

"I'm like barely pregnant, Mom. I think we should wait to shop for anything major. But, I will make a registry in a few months, for sure."

Margie selected a set of onesies with little animal prints on them. "These are just so precious," she said, lip quivering a little bit. "I'm so proud of you, Abigail. You are going to make a wonderful mother."

Abigail's stomach did a little flip and she felt slightly cold. "All I did was get knocked up, Ma."

"Oh shush, shush..." Margie put the onesies back and continued on. "A registry would be good, of course, but I want to buy most of the big things anyway, so... Tell me what you like. Do you like this style crib or more this?"

Abigail looked up at the display. A few were polished wood, one was more plastic looking, clean and white. "I like the dark brown wood," she said, pointing.

Margie clicked her tongue against her teeth. "Of course."

It was hard to tell, but Abigail almost thought her mother said that with some kind of tone. She didn't want to dig though; that chilly feeling was back in her stomach.

"I'd like to keep the nursery natural looking, simple. Not overstimulating. But, if we could find a bee mobile, maybe a few rattles, some simple soft linens, and some wall prints, that'd be really cute. Maybe a shelf. A flower night light. I've seen those online."

Margie stopped, hand on hip, in front of a display. It showed a pair of White parents holding a Black, presumably adopted, baby. Abigail looked at the poster which seemed to be advertising a brand of diapers, and to her mother. She opened her mouth to say, *It's good to see more diverse campaigns showing families of different kinds. It is 2020 after all,* but her mother spoke first.

"I am really glad you're going to be having a baby, and that I get to be a grandmother. It's just disappointing that no one is going to be able to tell it's *my* grandbaby."

"What do you mean?" Abigail asked, genuine confusion causing her brows to lower.

"I just can't see the baby looking much like us because of..."

Abigail watched her Mom swallow, then turn sharply away from the poster, moving toward a shelf full of bottles.

"Are you talking about how the baby is going to be mixed, Mom, because there are lots of mixed families, and people have all kinds of fami—"

"This set is adorable, don't you think?" Mom said, pressing a trio of silicone-nippled bottles with differing fruit patterns towards Abigail. "Do you plan to breast feed or bottle feed?"

Brain still trying to catch up with what in the world had just happened, Abigail took the bottles and looked down at them, studying the packaging so as to not have to look at her mother. She'd clearly changed the subject, but was that because maybe she'd realized she made a mistake? That was the only thing Abigail could reasonably assume.

"Yeah, they're cute," she said, handing them back. "And, I am going to try and breast feed, but also pump and let Jory do some bonding. They make these cool things that mimic the skin to skin experience."

"I see. I've never seen anything like that, but I guess another woman would be interested in breastfeeding, even if she couldn't do it herself."

The misgendering and mispronouning of Jory was not something Abigail would tolerate. She felt the clutch of anger tug at her gut and cleared her throat.

"Jory's not a woman, Mom, and their pronouns are they/them."

"Right, right... So, if sh—they, are not a woman, why are they interested in breastfeeding?"

"Breastfeeding isn't exclusively a woman thing, Mom," Abbi said, puffing her cheeks out around the rest of the words that wanted to come out. A whole queer feminist manifesto. She could have spent the next ten minutes explaining that trans men and nonbinary people breast fed sometimes, that people born without developing what was traditionally thought of as "breasts" could induce lactation with the right hormone and supplement treatments, and that there were cis women that found the idea of lactation abhorrent. But, instead she said only, "There are adoptive fathers sometimes who will do skin to skin contact and fake breast feed in order to establish a bond with the adoptive baby, and the mom will do it, too. So, there are all kinds of families out there. Just try to remember that, Mom, please?"

"Yes, yes, sweet girl." Margie reached up to pat Abigail's cheek gingerly. "I'm trying. Things just aren't how they used to be, and that's hard to take in sometimes."

"The world is constantly evolving."

"So it is. And we old people are just getting lost in the..."

She searched for a word for a long enough moment that Abigail sensed she was avoiding being problematic again.

Offering up a potential finisher to her mother's thought, Abigail said, "Lost in all the room to learn and grow?"

"Sure, that," Margie said with a nod. "Anyway, darling, just know that if you need anything at all for the baby, I will make sure it's there in a day. My grandbaby shall want for nothing."

With that, she was off down another aisle, snapping pictures of binkies and playpens, stuffed animals and wash clothes.

Margie was certainly a force. A force Abigail never could tell if well-intended or subtly destructive. Curious of the ultimate answer, she followed her mother mostly silent through the store, nodding or shaking her head at the various things pointed out. She was stunned when all she left with was a swaddling cloth, one with a baby bee pattern on it.

"This can be the first you hold her, his, their, little body with when they're born! Oh, I can't wait!" Margie said, handing Abigail the bag at the car before giving her a nearly suffocating hug. "Now, get lots of rest, stay hydrated, and don't be too stressed at work, alright?"

"Alright, Ma."

"I love you, my sweet girl! I'll see you soon. Send me that registry."

For better or worse, it would be the last time she'd see her Mother for a long time, though neither of them knew it then.

REASSURANCE

*Restoring or intending to restore confidence;
reducing or eliminating worry or uncertainty.*

JORDAN

The pregnancy was going pretty well by all measurable counts. There had been no need for a first ultrasound. Abbi had good bloodwork. No breakthrough bleeding. Not even that much morning sickness! There was just the single time she'd decided to eat leftover pineapple upside-down cake first thing in the morning and the sugar shock or something didn't agree with her. After a good purge and copious back rubs from Jordan, she'd felt much better.

Jordan had worried a little for a while after the bloodwork. Abbi had been off. Really off. After the puking and blacking out, she'd seemed a little more morose for a time, but whatever was on her mind, she'd brushed it off like there was nothing to it. She'd just

135

gone about fretting over the house, doing her nesting business. Once the tests were behind her, she'd seemed happy. Maybe happier than Jordan had ever seen her.

Abbi glowed with the pregnancy. She was amorous often, writing Jor poems in their lesbian notebook, sprawling sapphic pieces in cursive. Some were haiku, simple and romantic. Others were sensual, describing in such detail some intimate act they had or would perform that Jordan was left languid on the couch. It was certainly a new type of inspiration for Abbi. Pregnancy suited her in its own way.

Not typically a couple that celebrated commercial holidays other than Christmas (and being forced into family Thanksgiving), something felt different this year. Jordan wanted to do something special for Abbi on Valentine's Day, more than the sarcastic "Happy Valentine's Day!" they usually shouted at each other on the way out the door to work. This year it fell on a Friday, and Jordan was plotting something for after work.

"HAPPY VALENTINE'S DAY!" Abbi yelled from the bottom of the stairs, running out the door to drive to work.

"You too!" Jordan said, leaning out from the bedroom to wave. "See you tonight! Drive safe!"

Grabbing a bag full of Valentines, the kind kids give to each other in elementary school, Jordan took the bus to work. People were smiling on the streets. There was an abundance of flowers and people carrying red foil hearts. While Jordan normally found it kind of silly, there was definitely a shift this year. Was it just that they felt such joy? Were they projecting it out on others? Regardless, there was a lightness in the atmosphere that felt infectious. Maybe their attitude was making them see that more in the world, not that they hadn't been happy these past few years. It was just that now they felt happier than they thought was possible in the past.

At the hospital, Jordan skipped from room to room, big grins and big hugs for the kids that wanted them, handing out Valentines.

"Good morning, Johnny!" A high five and a Valentine card with cars.

"Makela! Happy Valentine's Day!" A big hug and a heart with a Princess & the Frog print.

"Carlos!" Finger guns and a PJ Masks Valentine.

This was basically how their morning went, checking in on all the kids currently on the unit, giving them their little treats and cards. The kids were always happy to see Jordan (one of the major perks of the job), but today that they seemed even more moved by Jordan's good vibes.

"You're extra extra happy, today," Sana, a five year old girl, asked. She gave Jordan a secretive smile like she'd figured out some big news. "Was the baby born?"

Oh kids and their complete lack of timelines. "Oh, not yet!" Jordan said. "But, you're right. I am extra extra happy!" They spread their arms wide. "I'm alive and I've got my family and you and it's Valentine's Day! Love is in the air."

Sana giggled, and Jordan about broke in half with the cuteness. Would they have a little girl? Of course, if they did, she could realize she wasn't a girl at all, and that would be fine, but Sana was too damn adorable!

But, then again, Carlos and Johnny, Tomtom, Peter, and Li were all adorable boys, each with their own charming quirks and of course, laughter. There really was just no going wrong. A kid was a kid, and they were all delightful.

Jordan ran a group in the afternoon where the kids got to make Valentines for friends and family and were delighted when two of the kids handed over Valentines for the Robins family. One featured a crayon drawing of a stick figure Abbi and Jordan, and a tiny poorly shaped oval for the baby (captioned as "bay b").

Another was three birds with little orange beaks and gray bodies with red tummies. "This is the robins family, get it?" the child said proudly.

Jordan didn't try to hide their tears. It was good for kids to see grown-ups cry, so long as it wasn't in an abusive way.

A dozen or more hugs, high fives, fist bumps, and finger guns later, Jordan left work to take the bus to the store. They'd decided to take a half-day in order to set up a surprise for Abbi at home later in the evening. Once back home, they clipped the flowers and arranged them in vases throughout the living room and dining room area, put out electric candles, and began setting out the spare Valentines cards they'd swiped from the kids' packs. They had written a little message on each.

"You're my princess and always will be," on a Disney one.

"I'd go anywhere with you," on one of the car ones.

"Will you be mine for all of time?" on a candy heart shaped one that said, "Will U B Mine?"

The messages continued like this, hidden in as many nooks around the room as Jordan could find, until at last they were satisfied she'd be finding them for the next few months.

On the dining table, they set out a bottle of sparkling cider, an alcohol-free bubbly alternative they could enjoy, a box of gourmet chocolates, and a homemade coupon for a "Free" full-body massage. They usually just focused on the feet after all.

Not too long after they finished setting up, their phone went off three or four times. It was Abbi.

"Can you take the bus to the school after work? I have a bunch of stuff I want to haul home today and I could really really use your help!"

Jordan looked back at the decoration. *Eh. It'd stay.* They clicked off the electric candles, tucked the remote in their pocket, then grabbed their house keys and coat.

"Yeah, of course. I'll be there soon," they texted back, then jogged down the street to the closest bus stop.

It ended up being around an hour before they arrived, but, by the time they did all the busses had rolled out for the evening. Jordan texted to let Abbi know they were there, and she came down to greet them at the door.

"Thanks for coming on short notice!" Abbi said, leading them up the stairs towards her classroom. "The kids were so sweet. They donated some of their favorite books from when they were little for the baby's room."

"Damn, what is it with all the sweet kids today?" Jordan said, biting their lip.

When they rounded the corner to Abbi's classroom, they could see a soft light glowing from beyond the door rather than the glaring fluorescents that normally beat down on the space.

Abbi rushed ahead to the door, turning and pressing her back against it, one arm twisted behind her to put a hand on the knob.

"I... Hope you don't mind this," she said, her gaze shifting toward the floor a moment. "But, it's done so..."

She opened the door, then stepped in backward through it, allowing Jordan to walk past her.

Inside, everything was as normal. Posters of parts of speech, famous authors, a cardboard stand-in of Maya Angelou, desks pushed together in stations, all of that. But, on Abbi's biggest most central bulletin board, usually featuring the current unit they were on, was instead backed in a brilliant blue paper with a border of cartoon guitars. Taking up the right half was a pastel drawing of Jordan smiling. The title read: "My Heartsong."

The rest of the bulletin board was filled with an acrostic poem, each line written in different handwriting. The first letters each line were made with construction paper, cutouts that had been illuminated with intricate illustrations. Butterflies, music notes, swirls, and dance shoes.

How can I describe a song in words? I can say it is

Endless, effortless, the way your heart sings to mine.
An aria, a symphony, my own pulse beating to the
Rhythm of your breath. Your smiles set the
Tempo, sometimes a slow dance and sometimes a
Salsa, and always a dance I want to do again.
One playthrough of this melody is not enough.
No, let it be an anthem for me to live by, and darling, I will
Go with you wherever your voice carries me.

How was Abbi supposed to follow the rhythm of Jor's breath when it was gone? They stared at the bulletin, feeling the lines of trickling tears form down their cheeks.

"I know we usually don't do Valentine's Day and all, but... It just felt different this year," Abbi said. "I hope you don't mind it. The kids helped me with it today, and I already am sad I'm going to have to take it down on Monday."

"I love it," Jordan said. "I love it. I love you. And you better be letting me keep this..."

"Well, duh," Abbi said, laughing. She wrapped her arms around Jordan's waist and tilted her head. "You deserve the world, you know. The whole world and then some."

"And so do you," Jordan said, then kissed her.

Finally, they found their breath again, there, hiding in Abbi's mouth. Life was perfect. As close to perfect as life could be.

But as March rolled around, Jordan couldn't help but start to panic. The hospital was abuzz with a new concern. They had caught wind in January that a pandemic was beginning to spread in China, and the first confirmed case in the U.S. had been little over a month ago in Seattle. But, that had all seemed far away. Now, though, the hospital was bristling with preparedness actions, planning for the worst case scenario. It was Johns Hopkins afterall, and the World Health Organization was releasing new guidelines daily.

"Abbi, I'm starting to freak out a little. I'm not going to lie. I know we can't trust Trump's word at all regarding the virus, but I didn't think this would become a thing. It's so weird that the hospital is starting to take all these measures even in the social work departments. They're talking about changing shifts and..."

"It's fine," Abbi said. "I'm sure it'll all pass, yeah? If things get worse, we'll prepare, but right now it's sorta all up in the air, right? We don't have any cases over here, yet. Hopefully it all got cracked down quick enough and we'll be just fine." She shrugged. "This is no different than when the kids were making fun of Ebola last year. Well, it's not funny, but you know what I mean."

Jordan wasn't certain. Abbi was hopeful.

March 6th, Abbi came home. She was clearly troubled, her voice mellowed and her usual enthusiasm gone.

"The superintendent of Baltimore County Public Schools released a statement today with all these measures in case of pandemic here..." she said, a touch frantic.

The pandemic, now dubbed COVID-19 by WHO and more colloquially as the Coronavirus, hadn't made it to them yet, but the reality was changing swiftly.

March 7th, the first reported case came through in DC and it was far too close to home. By March 12th, every single person they knew was fraying around their mental edges, and Abbi was starting to feel genuinely terrified. Jordan quickly put on their shining armor and stepped in to soothe her, trying to assure them both that all would be well.

It wasn't. On Thursday, March 12th, Baltimore County closed schools through March 27th. On the 14th, the first positive case of COVID-19 had made its way into Baltimore. On the 15th, *foraged.*, Atomic Books, and many of Abbi and Jordan's other favorite stores closed their doors to the public.

It was chaos. While Abbi called Dr. Diaz to find out about the first prenatal checkup, Jordan performed what turned out to be the unpleasant task of fighting through grocery stores to purchase essentials—frozen foods, canned goods, toilet paper, disinfectant. They had to go to three places to find everything they needed, and by the time they got home, they were stressed beyond their usual limits.

As soon as Jordan walked through the front door, Abbi said without looking, "Dr. Diaz says we'll just do my appointment via telehealth, and we'll schedule an ultrasound for April when we know more about what's going on with this COVID scare. We don't want to catch the 'rona." Once she looked at Jordan's face, though, all humor fled from her. "What's wrong?"

"It must be really serious, or at least people are taking it seriously," Jordan managed. "The stores are flooded with people. I got us what I could. It'll calm down soon, I'm sure." Taking a steadying breath, they tried to summon up the typical brave sorts of things they'd say. "Besides, it'll be good for you to get off your feet for a few days while schools are out. You can relax. Casual lesson planning. I'll still have to work, but that's alright. I wonder if the busses will run..."

They were rambling and they knew it, a tendency they had when things got too overwhelming. After dropping the bags on the kitchen floor, they immediately took to rubbing the hem of their jean jacket.

"Oh, Jory baby," Abbi said, crossing over to stand on tip-toes and rub Jordan's shoulders. "We've got this. We're both healthy and you're so strong, and it's going to be alright."

Jordan wasn't the type to spook usually, but they lost it now, crying into Abbi's shoulder. They sank to the floor together. Abbi held them gently, rubbing the back of their neck where their dark hair was clipper cut to a fade. Jordan eased into the feeling and was immediately grateful for their wife's loving touch. It worked magic for their tension.

"We've got this, Jory. We've got this."

The following Thursday morning, they tuned into the video appointment with Dr. Diaz.

"I'm sorry I can't meet you in person, yet," Dr. Diaz said, smiling awkwardly not at the camera, but somewhere off to the side.

The lack of eye contact was weird for both of them, and Jordan and Abbi exchanged humorous looks.

"You're a pretty healthy woman, Abigail. Your PCP sent over your most recent blood work and it looks pretty much exactly like it did when we took it. How are you feeling?"

"I've been struggling with appetite. Started to have some morning sickness issues recently."

"More like all the time sickness. Why do they call it that anyway?" Jordan said. "She used to be a vacuum, which I was rather fond of, and now she can barely choke down a salad."

Abbi reached across to touch Jordan's arm, her fingers touching so lightly they almost weren't there. "Don't you worry. These curves are just gonna get curvier, my love."

Dr. Diaz raised a single eyebrow, obviously not familiar with the two's typical banter. "Well, some people opt out of getting their first-trimester ultrasound anyway, so unless you have any major concerns, we'll go ahead and schedule an appointment with the ultrasound center we partner with for mid-April or so. Unless you've had any breakthrough bleeding or anything of the sort?"

"No, and pregnancy tests are still showing a clear positive," Abbi said.

"Not that she obsessively checks or anything," Jordan added.

Dr. Diaz chuckled at that. "Yes. It's your first pregnancy. These are perfectly normal things to think and worry about."

"When am I out of the clear for a miscarriage?" Abbi asked.

"Well... No one is ever completely in the clear until you have a newborn infant, but your percentage drops to a negligible level after the first six to eight weeks. You're also only 32 and other than being overweight—"

"Delicious," Jordan coughed.

"As I mentioned, you're in very good health from everything I can see," Diaz finished. "Did you have any other questions?"

"I don't think so," both Abbi and Jordan said together, flashing crazy eyes at each other with their synchronicity.

After the call, they were instructed to call the ultrasound center to schedule something for April. She would actually be about 4 months along at that point, and they'd likely be able to do the sex scan at that point as well. With that task tackled and as much reassurance as could be provided, all they had to do was keep moving forward until things were back to normal.

TILTING

The state or position of being sideways; slanted; biased; dispute or contention.

JORDAN

Quarantine. Jordan had never thought they'd live through such an unprecedented event. Were they back in the middle ages? Was this the next bubonic plague? How exactly was this going to impact Baltimore, and did it put the baby at risk at all?

Despite the slurry of questions this new reality raised, life felt much like it always had. Abbi was working from home now, but Jordan still went to work every day. The only difference was they had to go everywhere with a mask on. When they came home, clothes went right into the washer, they showered, and obsessively wiped down anything they'd touched along the way before allowing Abbi to greet them.

Margie, naturally, had called to ensure they were taking precautions and doing everything necessary to keep Abbi at low risk.

"Your Dad doesn't believe this COVID thing is real," Margie said to Abbi over the phone.

"Well, Dad is being downright dumb, then, Mom. Please be safe."

"I will, but you, too. We have no idea how this could impact babies. Jordan! I am guessing you're there."

Jordan covered their mouth to laugh. Abbi almost always put the phone on speaker. "Yes, Mom."

"Are you still having to go to work in all this?"

"Yes. But, the hospital might be one of the safest places right now. We're going above and beyond, I promise. And besides, my unit is pretty isolated from the rest of the hospital and far away from where they're taking any COVID cases. The kids aren't getting to see their families as much now. It's really sad."

"That's tragic," Margie said with a convincing amount of sadness in her tone. "Well, you take care of my babygirl."

"I will."

They'd been planning a big celebration for Jordan's 28th birthday with the entire friend group and polycule. However, with news of the quarantine, that couldn't happen now. They hoped they could host a "make-up" party once things calmed down a bit, but in the meantime they were going to play it safe.

Erica was beyond worried about the virus. She'd always had a somewhat frail constitution and the uncertainty of COVID-19 had her in an absolute panic. Alex called to cancel, and both Abbi and Jordan assured him it was totally okay and to give Erica lots of hugs on their behalf. Apparently, it was inducing an anxiety spiral that was leaving her more or less bedridden.

Josh was respectfully avoiding all contact, especially since he was deemed "essential" and still had to physically go into work. Jordan's co-workers and Abbi's teacher friends were also avoiding social encounters. It made sense, and honestly, Jordan was relieved. They didn't want Abbi and the baby at any more risk than they already were with Jordan going to a literal hospital every day for work.

Without a group of friends to entertain, Abbi instead lavished Jordan with several gifts (a new pair of sneakers, sunglasses, and a rainbow face mask). She cooked some of their favorite foods (they'd been tasked with going to the grocery store to get the ingredients, though). They ate grilled corn and homemade nachos with potato "cheese," taco spiced lentils, and fresh veggie toppings with virgin mint mojitos. As they munched and snuggled, they sat by the digital fireplace they'd purchased from The Home Depot just before the quarantine.

When they finished dinner, Jordan said, "The real gift this year is knowing the doc feels good about things and that we get to be safe here at home together. That we're not separated like some people are right now."

Abbi was gift enough. The rest of it was glittery icing on top of the cake.

"I can't imagine being distant from you," Abbi said. "Emotionally or physically. I'd be completely devastated. I know this is like, ooey-gooey lovey-dovey stuff, and totally based on attachment versus reality, but Jory, I can't imagine my life without you even for a second."

They kissed until Abbi fell asleep on Jordan's chest on the couch. The world outside was a scary place right now, but this felt safe. This just felt right.

Occasionally, they'd walk the streets together, peering in at the stores in sadness. The streets were far more empty, eerie given how Hampden was normally bustling on the weekends. Many of those walking wore masks, too, and gave each other the respectable social distance suggested in all the guidelines. The typically jovial, talkative streets were like phantoms of the past. Even the weirdness of the local suspects chasing and threatening to kill each other was absent, and the police that normally drove through the streets were not out in nearly as much force.

It broke Jordan's heart to see Abbi looking longingly in the window of Atomic Books. A sign printed in the window let them know they could order for curbside pick up, though, and that made Abbi a little less depressed. To both their relief, *foraged.* was still doing takeout orders, so they treated themselves regularly to meals from there as well as a variety of other places along the Avenue. They told themselves they were supporting local small businesses, even though it was a lot of money to get food out so frequently.

Jordan amped up the sweetness as Abbi began a new struggle with nausea, providing her with an endless supply of baby-safe herbal teas, and making all kinds of efforts to take care of her every need. Abbi's smiles pushed them ever onward, no matter how tired they might be from work and everything else. Abbi was exhausted with online school already, too, despite only being in "distance learning" mode for a handful of weeks. Staring at a screen until their eyes felt like they might liquefy was clearly not her preferred way of doing things, which made sense because she was so extroverted. That was one of the other many qualities Jordan admired about her—her endless energy for entertainment, education, and speaking up and out. Jordan was far more introverted and was grateful their work with the kids at the hospital was almost exclusively one-on-one. For all their bluster to Jim about being on boards, it had been mostly that. They worked more from the sidelines, influencing things in more subtle, soft-spoken ways.

"It'll all be over soon," Jordan said to Abbi as she groaned about needing to do yet another lesson online. "You'll be back in that classroom in no time, rocking your lit lessons in a way no one else can. You're a beam of golden sunshine, even if this all feels dreary."

But, April came swiftly and numbers of COVID cases were starting to climb. They received a call from the ultrasound center about a week out from the appointment stating only Abigail would be allowed in the building, but they would be permitted to use a cell or tablet to video call so that the "father" could be present for the ultrasound.

It was at that moment Jordan profoundly realized how much they wanted to be a part of this process with Abbi. At first, this whole situation had been bizarre, and Erica had quite a temper about it, too. But, there was more excitement all around now. It was good that Abbi and

Erica made up after the few tense exchanges early after the announcement, returning to the typical safety of their bond. With quarantine dragging on, though, they hadn't seen any of their close friends in over a month now. That was not only strange, but it felt isolating. The only plus side, which Jordan kept quietly to themselves, was that it made the experience of Abbi's pregnancy all the more precious. Only Jordan was really sharing in it, aside from texts, phone calls, and packages from Margie.

Jordan alone got to watch Abbi's belly slowly grow. Only Jordan got to compliment her glow and smooch her sleepy eyes in the morning. Only Jordan got to tend her morning sickness, bring her snacks, and rub her feet. These things weren't because she was hugely pregnant, but just because they were sweet things to do.

The level of intimacy between them was at an all-time high, despite the fear and stress surrounding the unknowns of the world as it contended with the additional dumpster fire. Jordan wouldn't trade the experience for anything—well, except maybe a 'rona free world. *Damn 2019 still coming after us*, they thought, glaring internally at how it was dubbed COVID-19 because the strain had begun in 2019. *We will never be rid of that damn year.*

So when the news hit that they wouldn't be able to physically go in and hold Abbi's hand, smiling next to her during the ultrasound, Jordan was admittedly disappointed. They tried not to show it too much, given how sensitive Abbi could be to their moods. They focused in on their gratitude that some doctor's offices were waiving the stupid no cellphones requirement and they'd at least get to experience it live. They'd also get the printed-out pictures and would give Abbi the biggest hugs in the world when she came out.

Since there was little excuse to dress up anymore, Abbi and Jordan went all out for this excuse to be out in public. Abbi wore her favorite flowy floral print dress with oranges and reds. It complimented her auburn hair. She wore a knit cardigan over top, gold dangle earrings, and a pair of slip-on kitten heels. Jordan thought she was the prettiest, purest being they'd ever seen.

Jordan put on their own favorite pair of high-top sneakers, rolled-up dark jeans, and bright orange button-up with navy blue suspenders. The two of them popped out even amongst the early spring blooming trees as they walked down the street to the car. Abbi got in the driver's seat without question because Jordan hated driving—part of what prompted them to move closer to Johns Hopkins in the first place.

As they arrived at the center, Abbi leaned over and kissed Jordan for a long lingering moment. "I love you, Jory. You're the best, and I'm sorry you can't come inside."

Jordan got lost in those gray-blue eyes a moment, touching the slightly upturned tip of Abbi's nose with a finger. "Have I mentioned lately how absolutely stunning you are?" They leaned in for another kiss.

"And have I mentioned you're the most handsome boi ever and I want to marry you again and again and again and..."

They distracted themselves with kisses for so long that when Abbi looked at the clock on the dashboard, she startled.

"Oh gosh, I'm late. Gotta go. I'll call you in a minute. I love yoooou."

Opening the car door but leaving the keys in for Jordan, she ran up the sidewalk. Jordan chuckled, watching her dress fly in the breeze, then sat there, waiting for her to call. They did their best not to feel too anxious, too excited, too expectant. It was hard to be their usual positive self with everything going on. The pandemic was well and truly a disaster now with the U.S. overtaking Italy in terms of number of deaths. Bernie Sanders had recently dropped out of the presidential campaign. So many people were out of work. Even Darrel was having to resort to selling coffee out of disposable cups, a thing he'd sworn never to do.

In a world with so much suffering at every edge, Jordan had Abbi, and that made everything okay. No matter how dire things might seem, they had their personified sunshine, Abigail Rose Robins: 32, she/her, educator and poet, smartest woman they'd ever known, and the world's future best mom ever. Jordan found themselves tearing up just thinking about how good their wife was, how absolutely amazingly, lucky in love they were. Their heart felt simultaneously like it might break free from their chest, and like it was perfectly cozy, nestled in their core all warm with butterfly kisses.

Rolling down the car window, they let in the scents of spring as they waited for their wife to call and began daydreaming.

Did they want to have a boy or a girl? They'd never let themselves really think about it, but now it was so close. They didn't care about gender in the slightest, but schools and society did. Maybe Abbi was right to think about homeschooling. They'd want to ensure their child knew with one hundred percent certainty that they could be whoever they wanted to be, believe what they wanted to believe, and pursue their dreams. But, Margie would have something to say about that, no doubt. Jordan felt the typical flare of rage that came with Margie crossing their mind, and brought their attention back to their breath. Margie wasn't ruining this special moment.

They'd do family things regularly once the baby was old enough. They'd create new traditions. Uncle Josh would be a regular feature. Maybe he'd get a puppy when the baby was a toddler, and they'd grow up together. Auntie Erica and Uncle Alex would shower the kid with little trinkets of affection and take them to the park down in Germantown. The world would be free of the coronavirus by the time the baby was old enough to go out and play, and maybe they'd put them in pre-school—a non-religious one.

Jordan's phone buzzed, and they practically leaped out of the car with a jolt, banging their head against the ceiling. Answering quickly, they saw Abbi was in a position laying down, staring up at the phone held aloft above her.

"Hey cutie," she said. "The technician is getting me all jellied up now."

Jordan grimaced. "That's... I dunno if that's sexy or gross."

"Me either," Abbi laughed, but her smile was hidden beyond her face mask.

"Alright, it's going to feel a little cool, but not cold. It's been in a warmer," Jordan heard the out of sight technician say.

"Did they make you put on one of those terrible hospital gown things?" Jordan asked.

"Mhm. It's all good. Don't want to get this lube all over my favorite dress."

"Heartbeat is good," said the technician. "Aaaand, here we are."

"Hold on, let me flip the camera around," Abbi said, and for a second Jordan saw her fingers in front of the screen.

From the car, Jordan watched the blurry footage, squinting to see the grayscale details of their future child's tiny body. The image was all flickering blacks and whites, senseless scattered forms.

"Here is the curve of it's butt. A little arm."

There is a reason trained professionals need to do this, they thought. It's like reading map topography for a place you haven't the faintest clue exists, let alone what the landscape was supposed to look like.

"I'm going to be taking some measurements," the technician said, her voice a little hard to hear through her medical mask. She clicked around on the screen, making what looked through the phone to be little dots along the ultrasound images. It was exciting, but boring simultaneously as Jordan had literally no clue what they were looking at. Abbi wasn't talking, and Jordan couldn't see their wife to stare at her, either.

Jordan came back to themselves as the technician asked, "Do you want to know the sex?"

"Yes!" Jor and Abbi said in unison, as they so often did with many questions asked by others. Despite not being able to see each other, they both bubbled into a swell of nervous giggles.

Jor swallowed down their general distaste for societal gender norms. The label didn't much matter to them and Abbi, but there were, unfortunately, plenty of people that cared. For all Jor's dislike toward cishet normativity in the world, knowing this child's gender would determine how the greater world treated them for the rest of their life.

"Well, it's a..."

There was a sudden, sharp pause punctuated by the technician leaning in toward the monitor. Even from the phone, Jor could see the woman's body language shift from the smooth confidence of one that knows their job to that of a person defeated.

Abruptly, the woman turned toward Abbi and the camera again, her eyes above her floral print mask filled with alarm and tears alike. She may have tried to speak, may have opened her mouth beyond the barrier, but no sound followed, save a harsh inhalation. She stood without a look back at Abbi and darted toward the door like a small bird fleeing a predator.

Abbi flipped the camera back toward her own face, her expression distinctly confused despite only being able to see her eyes. "What's going on, Jory? Is that normal before a gender reveal?" Her voice wavered slightly.

"I..." Jordan looked out the car window toward the front of the OBGYN center, frowning. "I don't know, Babbi. Maybe the kid's intersex or ambiguous and the nurse doesn't know what she's looking at." A hint of nervousness elbowed its way into their voice as they added, "Or maybe she's going to get the right colored fireworks!"

"Maybe." Abbi, either ignoring or missing the joke, sat up on the medical exam table. She shifted the phone so that Jor could better see her. "I suppose she'd be worried we'd be mad or something. She did assume you were my husband, and I think she was a little confused when I kept referring to you as they/them."

She pulled down her mask now that she was alone in the room, and a smile dragged up the corners of her lips as she shared this factoid. Jordan breathed again. It was going to be fine. As long as Abs was smiling, nothing in the world could be wrong.

Jordan heard the door swing open again, the creak and crack of the door hitting the wall stop unmistakable. Abbi didn't flip the camera around this time, so all they could do was watch her. However, she pulled her mask back down quickly as other people entered.

There was a shuffling sound—a rifling through papers, perhaps. The click of a mouse. The clearing of a throat. Abbi was staring at something, her ocean eyes wide with curiosity. But, that quickly changed to worry again, her brows lowering.

"Mrs. Robins," a different booming voice said, "Your child isn't viable."

"Isn't... What?" Abbi asked.

Jordan knew immediately Abbi wasn't asking because she didn't understand the vocabulary. She was asking because she just couldn't compute the reality of those words.

Though, Jordan couldn't either. They couldn't breathe. There was a well of absolute panic rising within them, especially knowing they couldn't be in there to process this with Abbi. Already they could see their wife's expression changing, shifting from one of prior excitement, hesitation, then mirth, back to absolute terror.

The other voice, presumably the doctor, went on. "She's got anencephaly, a neural tube defect. Her brain is exposed completely to the amniotic fluid and won't develop. I recommend terminating as soon as you're able, though of course they might view it as a non-emergency procedure since you could carry to term."

"But, even if I carry to term..."

"She won't be viable."

Jordan watched on, feeling numb and powerless, as Abbi's eyes registered pain, fear, and then the bottomless depths of sorrow. Her eyes were storm clouds shifting from the beautiful shade sky blue to a dismal gray as tears pooled and ran, darkening the edges of her cloth mask.

"Mister Robins, if I may," the Doctor said.

Wordlessly, Abbi handed the phone to the doctor. After a moment, Jordan saw his face, and he saw theirs.

"Oh, I'm sorry, Missus Robins," he said to Jordan.

"Mixter Robins, actually," they snapped back. They weren't sure if they were angry because of the doctor's assumptions about gender, the callous delivery of the news, something else, or all of the above.

"Ehm... Well, I regret to inform you that your wife won't be having a viable baby. There is a zero percent survival rate with anencephaly with most cases either being dead upon birth or passing on shortly thereafter."

"How is there a heartbeat then?" Jordan asked.

"It's through the placenta. The body functions perfectly, essentially, but once that connection is severed, the fetus's brain which is eroded, can't perform those tasks on its own."

"I see. What is the likelihood that you're wrong?"

"Based on the measurements of the chart, her head is severely underdeveloped. There is no skull above where the eyebrows would be. I'd say at best a five percent chance I'm wrong."

"Well, fuck your chances then. Give the phone back to Abbi."

The doctor handed the phone back to Abbi as wordlessly as she had handed it to him.

"We'll get you all cleaned up, Missus Robins," the technician was saying gently. Jordan could hear in her voice that she was losing a battle with tears. At least someone in the room was sympathetic towards Abigail.

"Baby," Jordan started to say, then winced at the use of the word baby. "Abs, it's gonna be alright. Let the—"

Abbi hung up the phone, leaving Jordan completely stunned and alone in the car. She had never hung up on them a single time. They tried calling back immediately. She didn't pick up. They opened the car door and tried to go into the building, but it was locked and the intercom buzzed with an apologetic affirmation that they could not come in.

"I've gotta get to her," Jordan screamed at the intercom. "My wife is in pain right now! I don't care about—"

They were once again barred contact as the intercom cut out with a faint static sound.

Jordan smashed a fist against the side of the brick building and paced from the car to the front door over and over and over, all the while furiously rubbing the hem of their shirt and chewing their lower lip until it was bloodied. Abbi was in pain. Abbi was scared. Abbi was alone.

They were alone, too. Terribly, utterly alone in what was the worst moment in both of their lives.

GRIEF

SHOCK

An automatic coping mechanism brought on by the body in an attempt to comprehend grief; if loss was unexpected, the feeling of shock may be heightened.

Abigail

The wells run dry. The tears locked up. And I might die. And I might die.

Abigail's head wasn't clear. It was static. It was agony. It was searing, crimson lava pain dripping down her spine, pooling in her belly. Burning. Burning. Poetry surfaced and swam. Drifted down the river of sorrow until they couldn't be heard anymore.

She'd stopped crying who knew how long ago. The nameless technician had guided her through getting dressed again after washing her stomach. She thought, anyway. Had that happened? What had happened? Who was the other person that had come into the room? A doctor? Doctor Diaz? No, Dr. Diaz referred her here.

Somehow, Abigail made it outside. Jor was standing on the sidewalk, their freckled cheeks streaked with tears.

My doe-eyed buck, blend of all the earth and stars and—

Abigail was consumed by Jor's arms, wrapped up in a cocoon and led to the car.

"It's going to be okay, Abs. It'll be alright. We're going to get a second opinion." Jor reached the passenger's side of the car and opened the door, not getting in. They motioned for Abigail to get in.

"No. I'm driving," Abigail said, her voice disconnected from her thoughts.

"Honey, that's probably not—"

She got in, the car still running, and put it into reverse with her foot on the break. Jor leapt in quickly.

"Honey, what are you—"

Abigail let go of the break and the car rolled backward. She didn't even check the rearview mirror. She knew there was no one there. Everything was empty, like her. She stared ahead at the road, and that was all she could do.

No. No. No. Her head grabbed at words. *Bow. Go. So. Low. I feel low. No.*

She couldn't bring herself to look at Jor again. Tears were never a good look on them, were they? Yet, they cried what seemed like 24/7. Pisces problems, seriously. She found herself feeling everything and nothing at once, her brain trying to reach out and focus on something, anything. Irritation at Jordan crying? Crankiness at a driver not using a turn signal? Nope. It was back to nothingness, emptiness, in the twinkle of a moment.

They got home. Abigail ripped off the dress and went to the shower. In the shower, she turned the water up so high her skin felt like it might melt off, and that seemed like the first good thing she'd ever felt.

She ate the ice cream. She ate the leftover pie in the fridge. She ate half a loaf of bread. Then, she puked. And puked. Then lay on the floor while Jor kneeled next to her, their voice moving in and out of her head like the sound of a fly moving in close to her ear, then flitting away. She chanced a look at Jor's face and found it worried. That wasn't alright. She looked away sharply, pulled herself up to a seated position, and found herself in the kitchen again.

Moments passed like this for days, in and out of conscious thought and reason, and then back into the abyss of despair.

A few days later, she found the Lesbian Book on the windowsill as she made coffee, no longer caring about caffeine intake. She heard Jor say something about a second opinion behind her, but ignored it. She heard Jor try to raise their voice, but ignored them. Instead, she heard the buzzing of bumble bees outside the open window and hated them.

Abigail pulled the notebook into her hands, her fingertips slightly bloodied from chewing them. Red smeared on the pleather, and she found it pleasing. That was nice. Blood meant life, but her baby wouldn't live, and then that thought ruined the rest.

Teeth clenched tight, she opened the book.

APRIL 16TH, 2020

ABBI, I KNOW IT'S IMPOSSIBLE TO UNDERSTAND WHAT'S GOING ON WITH ALL THIS. I CAN SEE YOU'RE NOT HERE WITH ME RIGHT NOW, AND I MISS YOU. I MISS YOU SO MUCH I DON'T KNOW WHAT TO DO. I MISS YOUR POEMS AND YOUR SMILES. THE WAY WE FINISH EACH OTHER'S SENTENCES OR JUST SAY THE SAME FUCKING THING. I MISS THE WAY YOUR FINGERS FIND MINE AT NIGHT. I'M NOT SURE IF WE SHOULD LOOK INTO SOME SORT OF INPATIENT PROGRAM OR NOT. I'M AWARE THE THOUGHT OF GOING TO A HOSPITAL IS PROBABLY SCARY FOR A MULTITUDE OF REASONS, BUT WE NEED TO DO SOMETHING

PLEASE TELL ME WHAT I CAN DO. ANYTHING. ANYTHING FOR YOU, BABBI, OKAY?

I LOVE YOU MORE THAN I KNEW I COULD LOVE, AND EVERY DAY I LOVE YOU MORE. MY HEART IS IN PIECES, AND I KNOW YOU HAVE TO BE IN EVEN MORE PAIN THAN ME. I HATE TO SAY THIS, AND I SWEAR I'M NOT TRYING TO

GUILT YOU, BUT I CAN'T GET THROUGH THIS WITHOUT
YOU. I NEED YOU BACK AS SOON AS POSSIBLE.
JUST TELL ME ANYTHING I CAN DO FOR YOU, AND I'LL
DO IT OKAY? — YOUR JORY

Abigail snapped the journal shut. "Jory?"

Jordan appeared as if summoned by actual magic. "Yeah, honey?"

"Can you make me a peanut butter and jelly and cut it in half?" Abigail said, once again hearing her voice but not being quite sure how it was coming out of her.

"Of course."

Jordan set immediately about the task, and when they turned back and handed Abigail a plate, all she could do was stare down at it. They had cut the sandwich in half, but in a weird almost puzzle shape. She distantly registered an awareness that Jordan was a jokester that thrived on smiles, but she couldn't smile. Instead, she handed the plate back to Jordan.

"Nevermind. I don't want it."

Jor cried. Abigail didn't look at them anymore, but instead went to the pantry, selected a bag of chips, and went to the couch to stare into oblivion for a while.

"Hey, Erica." Abigail registered Jor's voice and anchored for a moment into the present. There was a pause before they spoke again. "Yeah, she's not doing well."

175

Pause.

"I wish you could come, too. I don't know what to do."

A long pause.

"I'm trying. I swear to you, I'm doing everything I can, but she's just not responding to anything."

Pause.

"Mhm. Yeah. I..." Jordan choked out a sob.

Abigail pulled her face toward the direction of the sound. Jor's back was turned to her, their fade no longer visible on the back of their neck. Their hair was growing out. That was quarantine, she supposed, with a detached awareness that they were enduring life in the midst of a pandemic. *Huh. That's an odd reality.*

Off she went again.

Later, another day, maybe?

"Margie..." Pause. "Mom, I'm sorry," Jordan was saying. "I don't think it's a good idea that you talk to her at the moment."

Abigail could make out her mother's voice despite Jordan being in the next room over. "I demand that you put my daughter on the phone this instant or I will drive down there. That is my baby girl, and I am worried about her." She was yelling. Abigail hated when Mom yelled. It meant Dad was yelling, too. Anxiety flared, and she found herself struggling to breathe.

Then Jor was standing there with the phone held out, their face angrier than she'd seen in a long time. Their liquid amber-brown eyes were full of fire and spite.

"It's your mother," they spat, the venom in their voice actually bringing Abigail back to some semblance of life for a moment. Angry Jory was unheard of most of the time. Crying Jory. Worried, anxious Jory. Flow with the river, jokester, guitar playing Jory. All normal. This was a break in that, but not the good kind.

Fumbling, Abigail reached for Jor's phone and lifted it to her ear.

"Abigail?" Mom said.

"Hi."

"Honey, I am so sorry. I am so worried. I can't imagine how you must be feeling. Please tell me you're going to get a second opinion."

"Second opinion..." she reflected back.

"Yes, from another doctor."

"Oh. I don't know," she said, the numbness creeping back in like a volume dial being turned down in reverse.

"I'll make sure Jordan schedules an appointment for you. And if the second opinion is the same, well, you can look to get a healthy donor. This isn't your fault. All you need is a second chance and--"

Abigail didn't wait to hear the rest. She set the phone gingerly on the edge of the couch and got up, allowing her legs to carry her to the back porch. She'd water some plants. Plants were good. Plants were easy to keep alive.

For the first time since the ultrasound nearly two weeks prior, she crumbled and sobbed. Like a she-wolf, she found herself howling, lamenting the pup that would never be. The sensation was raw, the keening a foreign sound she knew she'd never heard before, and yet, it was welling up from her throat and bubbling out fresh with every breath. She sank into it, relishing in the bitter taste of anguish that surged through her past and present experience. All was lost, and yet it was not. It was all here.

Thoughts that hadn't been able to register before began to filter in. Uncertainty found its hold on her for the first time since the coronavirus had wedged into her life. *What does it all mean?* she asked within. *Did I do something wrong? What do I do from here? What did the doctor even say?*

Anencephaly. That had been the word. Jordan had gently tried to explain later, a day or two after the appointment.

Words flashed like cue cards in her head.

"Exposed to amniotic fluid."

"Not viable."

"Terminate."

She wanted to scream, but she couldn't. The tears were drying up again already, and though it hurt terribly to feel, she was glad she could for just a moment.

From inside, she heard Jordan yelling, but she couldn't quite hear what was being said. The words were drowned by the buzzing of bees that swelled up around her. She rubbed at her eyes, clearing the tears long enough to watch a small gathering of the striped insects dancing above the clover blossoms in the yard.

Life seemed like it was everywhere, but not in her. Her ears rang between the thoughts that threatened to take her under again, Jordan's ragged voice, and the sound of bees. So many bees.

Acknowledging reality was still too much to handle. So instead, she lay down on the grass, put her hands on her stomach, and willed herself to sleep.

DENIAL

When in denial, people try to avoid coming to terms with loss. It can manifest in many ways; denial of feelings or of the loss.

JORDAN

"First of all, if Margie opens her mouth one more goddamn time, I swear I might lose my mind," Jordan said to Erica over the video call.

"I feel you on that." Erica nodded at Jordan with a frown. "I'm so sorry this whole drama with her has to continue in the midst of... This." She waved a hand across the screen. "There is no manager to call to get her grandbaby back though. No refund for all those baby things she bought."

Jordan actually laughed at the Karen reference. "Mhm, shit that we specifically told her not to order, no less. Seriously though, Erica, when does this shit stop? Coronavirus is just getting worse, I hear there are like murder hornets trying to merc bees or some shit out west.

It's been two months and we're still in quarantine. I'm just glad Abs is sorta kinda coming back around now."

"But, what about you, Jor?"

"I'm fine," Jordan lied, swallowing down their feelings. Now that Abbi was talking to them again, even if casually, the last thing they wanted to do was upset her with their tears. They'd be fine. Afterall, it was Abbi that was really impacted by all this. She was the one with the baby in her body, leeching energy for no exchange.

Jordan had spent the last few weeks denying the reality of what was happening. They'd scheduled a second opinion, which really just looked like the other ultrasound center sending over the imaging they'd done. The specialist had frowned sadly over the telehealth call, and then confirmed the findings.

This can't be happening to my wife, was on loop in Jordan's mind. *That baby is healthy. That baby is healthy. Our baby is healthy.*

But, no matter how much they willed it to be so, it wasn't. They scheduled an appointment at Johns Hopkins for the termination on June 1st. May was already here. It was all happening so fast, and yet not fast enough.

"You alright there, Jor?" Erica asked.

Jordan blinked a few times, then nodded. "Yeah, sorry. I just don't want to accept that this is happening, you know?

That Abs is gonna need to go to a hospital. I wish we could have you there, but the hospital will only let in one person, and a professional support person if we have one, but we don't really need that." They bit their lip, crushing the need to cry down to a singularity before continuing. "I just feel like there's nothing I can really do, and I feel like an imposter because it's not really my baby, you know, but I'm over here—"

"Stop that right now," Erica said, her snapping like a rubber band pulled to full tension. "That child is just as much yours as it is Abbi's and she'd kill you if she heard you say anything otherwise."

"I... Yeah." Jordan took in a trembling breath. "Josh is in shock, too. I think he worries it's his fault somehow, but said he'd be willing to try again if the doc thought it's okay. But, God, I can't imagine putting her through this again, you know?"

"Yeah..."

"I just wish it was less clumsy for us sometimes. That I could ditch the turkey baster. Hell, maybe we should just adopt. Maybe I can suggest that."

"I wouldn't for a while. Let this play out." Erica gave Jordan an apologetic look, one corner of her lips quirking up while her eyebrows knit at the middle. "This is a lot, and you just need to go with it for now."

Jordan nodded. "Thanks, Erica. You're the best. I do wish we could see you."

"Me too. I hope this thing passes soon, but the way our numbers are climbing..."

"Not likely."

"Nope. Love you, Jor. Give Abbi a hug for me."

What Jordan couldn't bring themselves to tell Erica before they hung up was that Abbi was as prickly as a cactus in a mood. They hadn't kissed, snuggled, or even hugged since the parking lot before the ultrasound. A sense of foreboding snuck in, tightening Jordan's chest, and they decided to deny those feelings, too.

It was all going to be okay. As long as Abbi smiled, everything was okay.

But, she wasn't smiling. She hadn't smiled in what felt like fifteen years. She was now functioning "normally," taking care of things around the household. Cooking. Cleaning. Reorganizing. Asking mundane questions about how work was or what Jordan wanted to eat. She'd moved the multitudinous boxes of baby things to the attic, keeping them out of sight, though they knew not out of mind. There was no talk of the upcoming hospital visit. No talk of the pregnancy at all.

Whenever Jordan passed her in the house, she looked at them with an almost blank expression. They were roommates. No, strangers. But at least Abbi was always nice to strangers. She brought Jordan dinner after work and folded the laundry. Folded more laundry. Washed everything she could in the house. Scrubbed the toilets, sinks, showers. Steamed the carpet. When she put the Easter decorations away, ones she'd put out while still in the full swing of excitement about the pregnancy, she was silent and stony-faced. She murmured something about being glad there weren't any other holidays anytime soon, brushed her hands off on her leggings, and walked away from the attic like it left a bad taste in her mouth.

Whenever Jordan tried to approach her for physical contact, Abbi lifted a single hand, all five fingers drawn together in the universal "STOP" sign. Jordan respected her and walked away. Not caring what Abbi thought at this point, Jordan began drinking again. All the joy of making virgin drinks was gone, and even though the local brewery wasn't a place they could go sit, they could pick up drinks to go. They picked up a lot. It was fine, though. Abbi didn't seem to care if on the weekends Jordan passed out on the couch rather than coming to bed. They weren't really in much of a marriage these days, after all.

But, when not drunk, Jordan was lost in thoughts. They thought about their Mom's death when they were 15. How Dad had just shut down. All the life was gone from his eyes for a long, long time. Jordan had gotten so used to being at the hospital that the sudden lack of need to go had felt almost disappointing. It had been like a second home for a while. That was why it felt so natural to still be showing up to work during a pandemic. People might think a hospital was the most dangerous place to be, but for Jordan it was the safest. It certainly felt more like a sanctuary than this house did.

Jordan went downstairs from the office to find Abbi cooking dinner.

"Hey, Abs," they attempted.

"Hey, Jordan."

Abbi almost never called them their full name. It drove into their sternum like a knife, and they found themselves physically coughing as if actually wounded.

"You alright?" Abbi asked, almost sounding concerned.

"I'll be just fine." Then, mustering up the courage to take a massive risk, they said, "Do you think you'd like to maybe try a date night again soon?"

"No, thank you," came the stiff reply. "I made pasta for dinner." She turned and put a plate on the table for Jordan.

"Thanks."

Roommates. Strangers. Not even able to process this grief in the middle of a pandemic that left them little recourse other than the occasional escape for one of them.

The only real outs presently were walking around the sad city streets, or Jordan's time at work. And even when away, they couldn't help but live in constant terror that one day they'd come home to find Abbi dead. That's how it was day in and day out, until almost the end of the month when Jordan spotted the Lesbian Book on the window.

May 24th, 2020

This really is happening, Jor... We're going to have to kill our baby. I know I'm going to have to accept that because the day is almost here. I've gotten so behind at work after my leave, and I never thought I'd be this excited for a school year to be over.
I know you said you missed my poems. So here is one:

When do you replant something uprooted?
What if the roots are too damaged?
Do you plant a seed anew?
Do you let it go to dust?
Do you throw the whole pot into
the dump, toss the baby
out with the bath water?
How
does the seed stay alive

outside the life giving clay
it resides within?
How does the seed
exist when all it will do
is die an hour or two
after it finds itself free
Free

GONE

from the heartbeat of its mother Earth?
And another, because it's been in my head for so long now I don't
know what to do with it
The well's run dry, darling.
The tears locked up long ago
With the death of a dream.
I might die, I might die
With that dream.
Will you carry me into the waters?
Will you set the pyre alight?
Will you watch me go to ashes
Before it all goes dark?
Once upon a time,
You watched the sun rise—your lifeline.

And now I'm afraid that the lights all gone.
Heat death of the universe or some such nonsense.
What's nonsense is this situation.
Prisoner in my own body.
Let this sunbeam be carried off into the heavens.

That's it. I can't bear to write anymore. I know I can't show it right now, but I do love you. I just don't know what to do with myself, and soon enough, I'm afraid there won't be any self left to love you.

Love, Abigail

That use of her own name scared Jordan more than anything. The divide was clear, her mental state fractured. They knew from their own work that these sort of total breakdowns weren't unheard of in grief. Once again, the sense of being an imposter rose to grab hold of them, and they wondered if they were ever capable of loving a child if they were showing so little grief themselves.

That was silly. Of course they were grieving. They just needed to stay focused on keeping it together for Abbi. She was the one *really* hurting. That much seemed obvious. Standing in the kitchen, they read the poems through one more time, swallowed down all the pain that threatened to take over, and shut the book like they shut down their feelings.

That wasn't plausible forever though, and the reality was there was a third party that deserved some attention in this mess; if they couldn't do shit for Abbi, maybe at least they could see how Josh was processing things.

Jordan was cracking, a fraying, jagged edge of emotion. Being at home no longer felt comfortable; it felt suffocating, devoid of the warmth and light that had characterized it for so long. Silently, they slipped from the front door and escaped in one of their late-night jaunts down the empty street. As they walked, they slipped a cloth mask from their wind-breaker pocket, securing it over their nose and mouth. Despite the streets being mostly empty, they weren't taking any risks.

This fucking virus was making everything difficult. Josh, who they'd hung out with all the time, Erica, Alex—none of them had been able to come around and this was a time when they could use all the support that could be summoned. Reasonably, everyone was afraid, uncertain, and not willing to risk it. Under normal circumstances, Jordan wouldn't even ask.

But, this whole situation wasn't "normal." Jordan was the kind of person to say there was no such thing as "normal," and while that might be true, there were also decidedly things that were simply the opposite of normal. Using your BFF's spunk to impregnate your wife was probably not a typical everyday occurrence, but more certainly a worldwide pandemic where it was recommended you do not see your loved ones, especially if they were sick (or dying) was far from anything this generation had ever known.

A sob clawed its way from Jordan's throat when they came to a stop by a "CLOSED INDEFINITELY" sign. It was handwritten in bold sharpie, the black words punching out from the pale paper. The notice was taped from inside the coffee shop, the place where Josh and Jordan routinely hung out to shoot the shit most Friday mornings. Their standing "bro date." When was the last time they even saw him now? March 13th. The day news reached them of what was happening, imminently. Over two months. They'd never gone that long since they were on summer break back in high school, not even as busy body adults.

Jordan texted Josh.

"I can't take this anymore. Do u wanna meet me at the cemetery? We can mask n distance."

They paced up and down the sidewalk, toward and away from the coffee shop. In their mind, the four walls of that restaurant were now no more than a black square, struck off the map of possibilities. Seemed like everything was going that way. Swatches of space, time, people, and future dreams were wiped out in a few day's time. That'd been the pandemic's doing, of course. But, the void that was filing in now was all thanks to this tangled, fucked up fluke.

A vibration brought Jordan back to the moment, stopping them from spiraling further.

Josh replied, "Yea, i got you. be there in 10."

Jordan turned abruptly from the abandoned coffee place and took off toward the cemetery. Josh wasn't much of a texter, so there'd been little processing of all of the events. And, with Abbi's current state, Jordan did everything they could to not talk about her or the situation while they were in the house. So much restriction. On everything. All the time.

When Jordan saw Josh standing by their favorite tombstone, a gothic-looking Gargoyle, they almost ran to him for a hug. Remembering they couldn't, they swallowed the urge down alongside another rising sob, instead coming to a stop a good ten feet away. Their hands lifted as if they were opening their arms for an air hug, then fell heavily back to their sides.

Shaking their head, Jordan said, "Fuck, man."

Josh nodded back, his eyes the only visible part of his face beyond his bright orange Nike mask. "Yeah. It's about like that."

They stood there for the span of a few breaths, looking at each other wordlessly. It was so weird to not see Josh's face, a face that had become as familiar as their own. Was he frowning beneath the fabric? Smiling? Biting his lip in an attempt not to cry?

"How..." Finally Jordan spoke up. "How are you dealing with everything?"

Josh shrugged, his broad wiry shoulders lifting towards his ears. "I dunno, man. This whole thing is just weird. I mean it was weird to start with, yeah?" He let out a dry chuckle, paired with lifting a hand to rub the back of his neck.

"Yeah. I just..." Jordan paced a little, knowing they didn't dare get any closer to Josh. "I'm trying to make sense of it all, and I know that this was supposed to be *my* kid, but it was biologically yours and I feel like an ass for not talking to you about it before now. It's just Abbi's been so, you know..."

Josh nodded. "I can imagine. God, I can imagine." His brow collapsed in an expression of worry.

"So, how are you doing with it?" Jordan asked, pushing a little.

"I..." Josh took in what sounded like a rather shaky breath, his eyes closing. When he spoke again, his words came out in a breathless torrent, raw with worry. "I feel so guilty. Like, was this me? Was it my shit that caused this to happen? Is this why I'm ace, cuz I have some underlying biological drive to never have children because I'm just going to bring pain? I... God, I never woulda agreed to do this if I'd thought..."

"No. No. Stop." Jordan put a hand out, waving it as if cutting off the words. "This wasn't you. This wasn't Abbi. It was a fucking fluke, okay? We had no fucking way of knowing this kinda shit could happen. I'd never even heard of this defect before. It was rare enough that even the technician had to get a second opinion. This is *not on you*, okay?"

Slowly, Josh nodded, gaze downcast.

"Sorry," Jordan said, sighing out their tension. "I didn't mean to cut you off. But, I don't want you carrying this guilt, alright? And Jesus, this has nothing whatsoever to do with your sexual orientation. Dude."

Josh laughed, looking up at Jordan. "Yeah, you're right. It's an insecurity that comes up sometimes. Okay, a lot."

"I get you, but yeah, that's some heteronormative, compulsory sexuality bullshit programming right there. Nothing more."

They stood in silence again, just looking across the space at each other. Jordan couldn't tell if Josh was crying or dry-eyed. The moon was no more than a clipped crescent, offering no real glow. Other than that, only a few flickering street lights a dozen yards away offered any break to illuminate the dark.

"So, yeah," Josh started again. "I'm doing alright other than the nagging guilt. It's not like I was going to play a primary role in raising the kid. I was just gonna be cool Uncle Josh, and probably teach them to play sports." Shrugging again, he walked toward the gargoyle statue, reaching out to run his long fingers over its nose. "I'm sad for you and Abbi more than anything. The way I see it, I had no real stake in it other than being the donor."

"Did you feel used by us?" Jordan asked, a dormant fear rising.

"Nah, Abbi talked to me about it before I agreed to it. She was really assuring that like... It was okay if it didn't work right away, and also that if I didn't want to be the donor, she'd figure out a budget for getting another so long as you agreed."

"And what don't I agree to with her?" Jordan asked.

They could tell Josh was smirking. They could *feel* it.

"Rhetorical question!" they said, quickly.

"Mmmmhmmm." Josh laughed. "Some things never change."

"Maybe they need to."

Jordan pressed a hand over their mouth, feeling the smooth mask instead of skin. They suddenly felt nauseous, realization crashing into the pit of their stomach like a vodka shot, burning.

"You alright?" Josh asked.

Shifting their hand from their mouth to their forehead, Jordan felt to see if they might have a fever. Nope. Just a diagnosis of dread.

"It feels like everything is going to change. It already has, I mean, but even more so. It feels like something bigger is brewing, and I'm afraid I'm going to lose everything, Josh. We're good, right?"

"Wish I could say never better, but you and I know that ain't the case," Josh said. "But, we're good. As good as can be given everything."

"Thanks. When the whole world's gone to hell, it's good to know someone's got your back. Thanks for coming out here, even though I know you're trying to be as risk-free as possible."

"You're my best friend," Josh said. "That's what friends are for. I'm not gonna take the risk daily. You're not going to catch me buying take-out. But, it's been too long since we've seen each other, and I know none of this is easy."

"None of it," Jordan agreed.

They talked for about an hour more about what had been going on in life aside from constant tragedy. Josh was becoming quite the home chef, had taken up researching vegan cuisine and its health benefits, and was learning to make his own sourdough starters to try baking more. He was working from home now, trying to stay in shape, and generally keeping to himself.

It was so good to hear that life was still going on for their best friend. So reassuring to know that in the midst of everything, *someone* was finding some normalcy.

When Josh started shaking from the evening chill, Jordan said, "We better call it here. But, thanks."

Jordan lifted an arm, holding out a fist at a distance. From across the cemetery path, Josh mirrored the motion.

"Love you, brother," Jordan said.

"Love you back," Josh replied, dropping his arm. "Please take care of yourself. I'll try to text more, but you know me."

"Yeah, I do," Jordan said, smiling though Josh couldn't see. "And I get it. You take care of yourself too, and hopefully, soon something will change for the better."

It was a nice thought but born completely out of denial. Underneath their forced optimism, Jordan knew it was only going to get worse. How could it not?

ANGER & BLAME

After bottling feelings to avoid the inevitable, an outpouring of anger is possible. Anger may be targeted towards the situation, oneself, or others, as nothing can be changed in the present.

Abigail

As the day for termination grew closer, Abigail felt like she might crawl out of her own body and die somewhere dark. But, that's what her baby was going to do instead. She imagined the silhouette slipping down the drain while she lay in the bathtub, submerged up to her chin. Slipping. Slipping. It was all she could do to keep it together.

But, now that the day was drawing closer and reality was emerging, so too were the tangled emotions she'd managed to keep mostly dormant over the last hollow month and a half. She pictured Jor's face, so often wounded by her rejection, and all she could feel was angry. It was an unfamiliar feeling, one that she didn't like, nor know what to do with. She felt barbaric. The undercurrent of fiery fury ran through every thought now, and though she'd never had much of a temper or mean streak before, she felt her ability to keep such feelings muted slipping much to her own exasperation.

Did I really want a baby? Really? she asked herself, swirling her fingertips through the tepid water of the tub. *Did I bring this on myself somehow? Eat wrong? Pick the wrong donor? Not take enough vitamins? Not plan enough? This could have been prevented somehow. I know it. But, how? I'm going to be a baby murderer now, and I'm never ever not going to be a baby murderer.*

That thought alone was enough to drive the spike of hurt even deeper. She tried scribbling her feelings on a page. She tried watercolors which she had loved her entire life. She tried ripping the watercolors and the scribbled feelings to shreds and blowing them into the wind. Nothing budged the anger.

When Mom called, it was even worse.

"You could try again a few months after this is all over," Margie said on the other end of the phone. "Maybe," she paused, lowering her voice so Jordan had no way to overhear, "You just need to find the right man with the right genetics for you, you know?"

"Are you suggesting IVF, Mom? Because that's insanely expensive."

She could hear her mother grappling for a reply, the pop-pop of her mouth opening and closing. "I mean, I will gladly make sure to send some money your way if IVF is the right choice for you. But, if things don't work between you and Jordan, you could find a man with more... similarities to you."

"Things between Jordan and I are fine, Mom," she lied. They weren't, but they also weren't as bad as they could be. It wasn't like Mom and Dad's relationship.

"You always did follow your heart, dear, no matter how it guided you. That's something to be admired, I suppose."

When they hung up, Abigail somehow felt even angrier at everything, including herself.

The evening after that latest call with Margie, Abigail and Jordan sat at the dinner table. Jordan was rambling on about the latest measures the hospital was taking, attempting to assure Abigail without directly saying it that they'd be safe when they went in for the procedure.

"I don't fucking care, Jordan. Please shut up. Just drink your beer and be quiet." Abigail knew it wasn't like her to swear much, let alone at Jordan, but again, she couldn't summon a single compassionate iota in her being. "My child is already dead to the world, and I don't care if I go out with her."

Abigail stood and pushed the chair back in so violently it sent the slightly off-the-edge plate shooting off the table. As it collided with the cabinet with force, shattering into jagged shards all over the kitchen, Abigail watched Jordan devolve into their all-too-typical tears.

Fuming and silent, Abigail watched her tearful spouse shakily rise from their own chair and go to get the dustpan and broom.

"No! Leave it!" she shouted. "Just leave it! I will deal with it. This isn't your problem to deal with. This isn't your baby that's dead."

Somewhere inside, Abigail acknowledged she'd just crossed some sort of sacred line. Yet, she pushed on even as Jordan turned their tear-stricken face to look on at her in shock.

"Abbi," they tried to start.

Abigail cut them off, her words coming in a torrent now as her temper flooded completely over, crashing against Jordan with a visible force. Each new word was another shove, and Abigail relished in it—relished in someone else feeling even a semblance of the pain she felt.

"No. Don't even start in on me. I fucked up. I did it all wrong, and now I have to deal with the consequences. Maybe if I'd made smarter choices in life, I wouldn't be in this situation. Maybe if I'd married a man like my parents wanted me to, or if I'd just been a recluse in the woods somewhere and hid my sexuality from the world. Maybe this is God's punishment for me being gay. Who the fuck knows. I certainly don't, but I bet Mom is thinking this is exactly the punishment I deserve for my sins, even though the expense is her own biological grandchild."

She watched as if in slow motion, Jordan stopped what they were doing, put down the broom and dustpan, and walked out of the room.

"That's RIGHT," she screamed after them. "Just walk away! Walk away from me when I am in the worst pain of my life!"

The house actually rattled as Jordan slammed a door somewhere.

Good, Abigail thought as a laugh escaped from the confines of her throat, snaking out to make its poison known.

She stared after the direction Jordan had gone, then yelled, "GOOD!" after them.

It felt liberating to tear into someone else. It shouldn't, part of her thought, but she quickly and decisively shut that part up, locked them in a mental lock box, and drowned them in an ocean.

News of George Floyd's murder gave Abigail a temporary place to put her anger. Yet another Black man wrongfully killed in the name of what? Suffocated to death. Literally suffocated to death over what would have amounted to $20.

Another victim. Another excessive use of police force. Another day that racism prevailed.

It made her feel ill on every level—spiritually, emotionally, mentally, and physically drained. Jordan was distraught as all over the U.S. protests, marches, and other demonstrations began rippling across the nation. There was going to be a protest on the 29th in downtown, Jordan said, tiptoeing around Abigail like she was a monster that might snap their head off at any moment. But the sorrow in Jordan's eyes as yet another of their race was the open target of police softened her.

"Hey," she said, walking up to Jor in the kitchen, and wrapping them in a hug. The first since the ultrasound.

"Jory. I'm sorry this is happening... Especially on top of everything."

For all her upset, all her desire for violence against everything and everyone around her right now, she couldn't possibly begin to imagine what pain Jory must be going through.

"Thanks," Jordan said, clutching Abigail to them as if they let her go, they may never get her back.

Their fear wouldn't be that far off, really, Abigail knew. She was on the precipice of self-made disaster.

The two had their first Friday night date night in months by attending a protest at the Inner Harbor in Baltimore. Around 7, they blocked traffic on Light Street and marched on City Hall. Abigail felt free, marching upfront, using her White body as potential protection. Had she been truly pregnant with a viable life, she knew she wouldn't have done it. But, she wasn't, and so she put herself out there secretly hoping if something was thrown or shot at the crowd, she could take it for them.

"Could 2020 be any worse?" Jordan asked.

"It could, yeah."

"Do I want to know how?"

"Nope."

They left it at that, walking hand in hand home after the demonstration was over.

Abigail knew as soon as she saw the Lesbian Book that what followed wouldn't be good. She took it down, paused to grip the edges, and contemplated if she should really pursue reading it. Trying to steady herself, she opened it up and began to read.

MAY 30TH, 2020

I AM GRATEFUL YOU WENT TO THE PROTEST WITH ME. I'M GLAD MY WIFE IS AN ALLY. IT FELT GOOD TO BE OUT THERE IN THE WORLD WITH YOU AGAIN. THIS IS A SAD, TERRIBLE WORLD WE ARE IN, AND IF... GOD I DON'T KNOW IF I WANT TO WRITE THIS, BUT I'M GOING TO, ANYWAY... I AM KIND OF GLAD THIS CHILD ISN'T GOING TO HAVE TO SEE THIS FUCKED UP WORLD.
I'M SORRY IF THAT HURTS, BUT I'M ANGRY, TOO, AND I NEED TO SPEAK MY MIND SOMEWHERE SINCE I CAN'T SEEM TO SPEAK IT DIRECTLY TO YOU.

HOW YOU'VE BEEN TREATING ME ISN'T OK. I WANT TO PRETEND IT IS AND JUST MAKE PEACE WITH HOW MUCH PAIN YOU'RE GOING THROUGH.
I KNOW YOU CAN'T ACTUALLY MEAN WHAT YOU'VE BEEN SAYING LATELY. IT'S NOT LIKE YOU
THE SWEARING, THE ACCUSATIONS, THE EXPLOSIVE ANGER. I KNOW YOU'RE IN IMMENSE PAIN, AND I'M NOT GOING TO BOTHER GETTING INTO HOW MUCH PAIN I AM IN, TOO, BECAUSE I KNOW IT WON'T HELP.
BUT, I WANT TO SAY IT'S SIMULTANEOUSLY OK TO FEEL HOW YOU FEEL, BUT NOT TO TAKE IT OUT ON ME. AND IT

IS REALLY NOT COOL FOR YOU TO SAY THAT BABY ISN'T MINE.

THAT'S WHAT WE AGREED ON, AND JUST BECAUSE YOU'RE IN PAIN DOESN'T MEAN YOU GET TO GO BACK ON THAT.

WHAT HAPPENED TO ME BEING YOUR ROCK AND YOU MY SUN? YOU KNOW, I'M PISSED, TOO.

I AGREED TO GO INTO THIS ADVENTURE WITHOUT A SINGLE MOMENT OF HESITATION, AND I DON'T WANT TO REGRET NOT PAUSING TO CHALLENGE YOU

THIS WAS CRAZY. IT WAS. BUT, I DON'T REGRET IT SO LONG AS WE CAN COME BACK AFTER THIS STRONGER THAN BEFORE.

YOU'RE MY ABBI BABBI, AND I LOVE YOU. I'LL ALWAYS LOVE YOU. NO MATTER WHAT THIS UGLY WORLD THROWS AT US, I'M GOING TO KEEP ON LOVING YOU, BITCH. YOU READ THAT? READ IT AGAIN. I'M GOING TO KEEP ON LOVING YOU, BITCH.

BUT PLEASE, DON'T EVER SAY THIS BABY ISN'T MINE AGAIN. THAT HURT WORSE THAN YOU WOULD BELIEVE, AND IT JUST SPITS IN THE FACE OF THIS ENTIRE PARTNERSHIP WE'VE BUILT UP OVER THE LAST SEVERAL YEARS.

I LOVE YOU — JORY

Abigail finished reading the entry, trying to monitor the up and down of her own emotions. Talk about a roller coaster. Guilt. Shame. Pain. Anguish. Anger. How dare Jordan write something like this only two days before she was going into the hospital to terminate. They were supposed to be her number one support, but this wasn't support. Since when did Jordan draw such solid boundaries? Since when did they speak up for themself? Was now the time to start?

Despite all the goodness and support that existed once in her, she couldn't find it. With a frustrated cry, she turned and threw the journal into a nearby wall. A picture frame with a photo of Jory and her on their fifth date, the day after they moved in together, shook with force, then fell. The glass shattered.

"FUCK!" she shrieked, just as Jordan came rushing into the room with a beer in hand.

Abigail wheeled on her partner, panting as her heart rate kicked it up to well over the active cardio zone, and all she had to do was stand there.

"All I'm good at doing is breaking things! Wrecking things. Fucking it all up." Her vision was coming in and out, blinking away with splotches of blackness as her heart pounded a trance drum in her ears. "I do mean it. I mean every word. I hate this stupid little life we've built. I hate being gay. I hate that my parents are racist pieces of shit and so is our society. And I hate you, Jory, for always sweeping in with your social worker bullshit at the wrong fucking time, staying stoic when I don't need you to, and breaking down when I need you to be strong."

Jordan stood mighty as the Statue of Liberty, one hand on their hip, the other lifting slowly to sweep through their ever-growing mess of dark curls. They took what appeared to be the world's longest breath, held it until it was clear they'd burst, then forcibly exhaled.

"Either you sit down or you clean that up. Make your choice," Jordan said, their voice profoundly flat, razor-thin black ice.

Abigail stared at them in commingled awe and anger. Jor had hit their own edge, it seemed. She was simultaneously proud and outraged. She opted to sit down, not wanting to look at the picture of that beautiful date to Druid's Hill Park. There could be no good memories now. It was all gone to the abyss, lost to the sea along with any shred of humanity Abigail felt she had left.

She was shaking when they entered the hospital, both of them wearing masks. They'd been able to get rapid turnaround on COVID tests from the hospital staff since Jor worked there, though they'd still been insanely uncomfortable. No one liked having their brains jabbed out with what felt like a spiky q-tip.

The hospital room, to its credit, was private. As soon as they arrived, a nurse with a heart-shaped face led them to where Abigail would give birth, giving them privacy to have her change and get settled in.

Abigail undressed and slid on the hospital gown. In response, she felt a rush of pain spread out from the center of her chest. Suddenly, she was off balance as images and sensations from the ultrasound returned in flashes.

Jor rushed to her side and helped her stay upright, assisting her in getting onto the cot. Their powerful arms, even atrophied from time without a gym, barely needed to exert effort to guide her.

"You alright?"

"No. Not even slightly."

"Do you need anything? Water?"

It made Abigail even angrier that somehow despite all her barbed words and seething tongue, Jor could still be so gentle. But, she needed it now, nonetheless. It felt bad to call on them after she'd been such a righteous bitch, but it was what it was.

"Water please."

Jor even smiled when they brought the cup over. The shame made Abigail's ears go red. She tried not to look at

Jordan, tried not to love them. Tried to shut it down. All the feelings. Today would be too much, and she already knew it.

As usual, her bad feelings were on point. The doctors and nurses, kind as they were, tried in wholehearted vain to get the drugs that would help Abbi go into labor to work. The ones causing contractions were, but the ones meant to help her dilate were not.

"We're going to have to use a special tool," one of the nameless doctors said to Abigail, gently. "They're called laminaria, a type of seaweed. We insert them into the cervix to assist in dilation when the other drugs don't ripen it properly."

"Is it painful?" Jordan asked.

"It can be... uncomfortable, yes," the doctor confirmed. "We can give her morphine or other pain killers to help if it gets too much."

The procedure to insert the laminaria alone was uncomfortable. They opted for three, hoping the manual stimulation of dilating her would push her the rest of the way over. Abigail felt immediately nauseous, but powered through. She'd never liked gynecological exams, and this felt like that on steroids. Jor squeezed her hand gently through the process.

"I bet you'd rather be at home with a cold drink right now," Abigail said, squirming a little.

"There's nowhere in this universe I'd rather be than at your side, kay Babbi?"

Over the next few hours, the discomfort bloomed in her lower body. It was gradual at first as the seaweed sticks swelled, taking in the moisture from her cervix. Early on a dull ache, it had a sudden onset of pain like being penetrated with a hot iron rod. The torment made her cry out in guttural agony, and she threw up all over her hospital gown.

Jordan cleaned her up, wiping her down and helping her change. "Can we get her some morphine?" they asked when a nurse came in to check on the progress.

Abigail drifted off to sleep briefly as the pain dulled with the drugs. When it was time for a second round, however, they had no effect save making her nauseous enough to hurl again. Fortunately, Jor was there with a bedpan and a cool towel this time.

"Thanks," she said, but it was all she could manage as her head babbled off soundless syllables of nothingness to try and cope with the physical misery. The mental was all but left behind, wiped out by the singular point of focus that was her traitorous vagina.

Unfortunately, when the doctor came in to check her progress, she wasn't nearly far enough along. When Abigail heard the proclamation "We're going to have to insert more," she openly wept.

How could a body hurt this much? How could something that once gave her pleasure save for that week or so a month now fill her with such affliction? She wished she'd never been born with a uterus. She wished she'd never been born at all. Her body was being ripped in half from a seam midway down her body, she was sure of it. The cleft of her lower lips traced a line straight up her form and split her into two pieces. Right and left hemispheres separated. No longer a complete picture of life. She was as fractured as the photo and frame on the living room floor.

She was incoherent. Babbling. She saw Jordan's face swimming in and out of her vision, unaware of its orientation to time or relative space. Yet, she couldn't tell basic things anymore, like what facial features were or why she'd once found Jory so beautiful. Basic building blocks of life meant nothing. The passing of hours meant nothing. The only thing that existed was the convulsions of each contraction which caused the torture to cut deeper. Ripped. Sliced. Lacerated. There was no word with a connotation intense enough to describe it.

Although terrified of needles, eventually the sense defying pain won out, more powerful than any fear had ever been. "Please get me an epidural."

As the nurse left, another nameless, faceless doctor came in to check her status.

"I think you're dilated enough," came the decree, and Abigail could have wept yet again with relief.

The luminaria were removed one at an excruciating time, each one draining her of color until her skin was porcelain. At last, that part was over. She could actually take a breath again, and did so, shuddering.

"If you want to go ahead, you can try pushing."

The nurse walked in with an anesthesiologist just as Abigail gave her first push. She felt her kegel muscles, sensed her pelvic floor, and pushed again, again, then felt a rush of warmth, tenderness, and reprieve. She knew she'd done it.

"Well done," the doctor said.

Abigail looked down toward the end of the bed to see the doctor with some sort of sharp metal object and a silver tray on which lay a jelly-like ovular shape. She could barely make out the pale outline of her child—their child, within. Jordan's face was drenched in sweat, their jawline even harsher than usual as they grit their teeth.

"Do you two want to hold the baby?" the doctor asked, puncturing the amniotic sac carefully.

"I do," Jor said, voice breathless. "But only if Momma doesn't want to first."

"You go first," Abigail said, feeling faint suddenly. Leaf trembling in a crisp breeze. Held breath.

The anesthesiologist left, leaving the nurse to help the doctor clean up the very small baby. When they were done cleaning her up, they put a small knit hat on her head to cover the smooth exposed brain matter. Abigail, still woozy, watched them hand her off to Jor.

Jordan was trembling as they held the tiny child, their long-fingered hands stacked one on top of the other, cupping the swaddled form effortlessly.

"You're beautiful," Jory choked.

Abigail sputtered as she strangled herself on a sob. She had been cruel to ever accuse Jory of not being this baby's parent. They were. They were that and so much more, yet that hurt more than ever to acknowledge.

Moving over to the edge of the bed, Jory knelt beside Abigail and laid the baby on her chest.

She felt numb as she stared down at the tiny form. Unwrapping the swaddling slightly, she looked at the minuscule hand. Her hands. Her skin was the color of pink roses with veins showing through, not fully developed at less than six months gestation. But, she was an echo of what she might have been, her face showing the line of a chiseled jaw to be.

That made Abigail lose it. She wept as she placed a finger in the tiny hand, tracing the edge of her little baby-doll face with the pad of her thumb. It was too much to take seeing her child, made of her blood and cells, dying. Or dead?

"We couldn't detect a heartbeat," the doctor said, reading her mind.

It was hard to believe. The last vestiges of life were lingering, she swore, as the petite fingers seemed to close around the tip of hers.

"What will we name her, then?" Jordan asked, seeming to find the strength Abigail couldn't.

"I always wanted a Joscelin," she said, practically suffocating with the effort.

"After your favorite book character. Of course. I like it." Their typical support was back as if it had never been challenged. "It's nice and gender-neutral, too. She, they, or he, or ze, or whatever pronoun they'll use in the great beyond, could be Jos, Josie, Joscelin, Lin... It's a great name."

As Jordan forced a smile, Abigail did her best to mirror the effort.

"Yeah. A little queer angel baby."

Nope. She lost it again, and so did Jordan.

They were left alone for about an hour, the nurse drifting in only occasionally to check on them. Jordan took a few photos with their phone before the nurse came in for the final time.

Swallowing down the fist of emotions battering at her throat to spill out, Abigail closed her eyes. When she spoke, her voice only waved once. "We'll donate her to science. So maybe another couple won't have to go through this."

"Thank you," the nurse said, taking the bundle away from Abigail with an almost reverent touch.

"Bye Josie," Abigail whispered, lifting a hand to reach out for her as she was taken away. Her fingers grabbed at the air, just like she'd reached out for Jordan on the brick wall the night she'd suggested this insane scheme.

The world was loud. Deafening. Abigail felt off-center as Jor led her to the car. She couldn't even protest when Jordan drove this time. She was bleeding into the oversized diaper pad she'd been given, and her legs were as shaky as pillars made of sand.

When they got home, Abigail gave in to her own exhaustion. It was late. It had seemed like a forever ordeal, and one she knew she never wanted to live through again.

"I'm letting everyone know we're home safe," Jor reported, helping Abigail get comfortable in bed. They lifted their phone, typing into it furiously, then sat down beside her. "How ya feeling, champ?"

"I'm... Here," Abigail said weakly. "That's about it. I'm glad it's over, and not glad. That pain, Jory..."

"Looked pretty bad."

Abigail nodded, jumping slightly when her phone rang.

"It's Mom," she said, looking down at the screen.

"Don't answer it," Jordan warned.

"How can I not?"

Ignoring the recommendation, she swiped the screen to answer the call.

Margie's voice came through, distraught. "Abigail, I can't believe they wouldn't let me be there to see the birth of my own grandchild." A dramatic sniff followed.

"I'm sorry, Mom," Abigail said. "It was the hospital's policy."

"I wish you'd argued for me to be there. I'll never get to hold her now. What did you name her?"

"Joscelin."

There was a pause. "That's... Unique. What did the doctor's say? When can you try again?"

Abigail met Jordan's eyes and wavered slightly. "I don't know, Mom. They said I could be bleeding for like a month or so."

"Even though you don't even have a baby to bring home... It's a rotten shame. But, it'll probably be fine next time, right?"

"I don't know, Mom," Abigail said, watching the shifting of Jordan's expressions. It was growing dangerous, the air thick with pressure from all sides. She was teetering, with no concept of how to keep balance.

"Well, I've been looking into potential donors for you all," Margie said. "The Seattle Sperm bank has lots of promising candidates with strong German heritage like ours and..."

"Alright, that's enough." Jordan plucked the phone right out of Abigail's hand, pressing the red End Call button.

Their face read rigidly, resentment and regret in bold strokes of the brush. When they spoke again, Abigail's stomach plummeted to the bottom of the ocean to retrieve all the emotions she'd abandoned.

"I'm done with your Mom, Abbi. And if you don't stop giving in to everything she says, I'm done with you, too."

BARGAINING

In this stage of grief, one may try to reason with themselves that by doing something differently, it could bring a loved one back. Often, irrationality appears during this stage, and the word "if" surfaces frequently as thoughts explore what could have been done differently.

JORDAN

Jordan regretted the statement as soon as they watched Abigail's already exhausted, worn face fall into despair. She'd just lost her child, and now they were guilting her about her mother. It was the wrong time.

"I'm sorry, Abs," they started.

"It's okay. It's fine. I've been a bitch, and you're right, I think. Can I just sleep now? I'm beyond tired."

"Of course, Babbi," Jordan said, rising to tuck her in. "I'll be downstairs if you need me. You can text me or just holler."

As they left the room, they couldn't stop picturing Abbi's dead eyes as soon as they'd said they were done with her if she didn't stop with Margie. It was a haunted look, one rife with the remnants of all the pain she'd just experienced. The enmeshment they'd often laughed about having, the "Lesbian mind-meld," had been absent for the last few months. But, at the hospital Jordan had felt it again in a visceral way, waves of Abbi's pain emitting from her with every shift of her body, every heave, every closing of her eyes and gritted teeth. The absolute hurt that coursed through her had been palpable. Jordan had definitely not enjoyed it from the outside; they were nigh on hysterical just thinking about what it must have been like to live the fully embodied experience.

There was no way Jordan was ever going to let Abs go through that again. Whatever that meant, they weren't going to let it happen. They'd burn the house down before they agreed to such a hasty plan again, if they ever agreed to try for another pregnancy at all.

Angry, confused, looking for something to offer the Gods for a reprieve, Jordan threw away all the alcohol in the house.

"Please, if you exist up there, whatever power in the universe is listening, please just let us have a happy life together."

Was alcohol to blame in any way for this? The parts of Jordan that held their clarity knew it was not. Jordan didn't like how they felt binge drinking in prior months when Abbi was cold. It hadn't been a positive way to cope. They regretted it, wondering if they'd just maintained their support through the whole ordeal, Abbi would be alright.

Maybe if I'd stalled... Talked it out. If I had been braver about standing up to Abs in the first place. If I wasn't such a pushover...

Their head was heavy with these what ifs for the next several days. As news of more police brutality made headlines, and Abbi stayed in bed for days on end, tearful and in pain, Jordan felt livid, lonely, and listless. Jordan was at a loss even more than when Abbi had been angry at everything, even more than when Abbi had been distant and prickly. Now that it was all over, they wanted Abbi back, but also had to accept that she was feeling beyond empty in the aftermath of everything.

Erica was left to help them rationalize again.

"Do you think if I just work harder at showing Abs how much I love her that it'll help?" Jordan asked on video chat.

Erica pursed her lips, planting her chin in her hand on her desk. The webcam rocked a little. "I wish I could say there was anything you could do that would help, but Abbi is isolating from everyone right now, Jor. You, me, Alex, Josh. We're all worried, and I already know you're doing literally everything you can. There isn't much more you can do but give her the time and space she needs."

"What if..." Jordan swallowed that thought down. They didn't want to think about the possibility that their relationship might not survive this. "What if," they said instead, "I am the one that tries to get pregnant next time?"

It was a thought they'd been wrestling with. They were in better physical health than Abigail overall. Not that her health had necessarily caused the neural tube defect. It could be so many different things. Low folic acid, an inability to absorb nutrients properly, environmental factors, genetics, obesity, uncontrolled diabetes, medication, or just a simple fluke. If they both went on a hardcore diet, exercised, took daily vitamins, and generally prepared for it, maybe Abbi could strengthen her chances of carrying a healthy baby to term, if that was what she wanted. Regardless, this was not her fault.

But, the option for Jordan to try instead was one that bypassed the hard work for Abigail.

Erica was silent for a long time on the other end of the call, just staring directly at her screen—clearly studying Jordan's face rather than making fake eye contact with the camera. After pursing her lips and relaxing them, pursing them again and relaxing them about twenty times in rapid succession, she shook her head.

"No, Jor. If there is anything I know about you, that is one hundred percent just you trying to accommodate for Abs. You've never wanted to carry a child, and I'm guessing you're only bringing that up because right about now you'd do anything to get Abbi back to her normal self, even if it meant sacrificing your own body you've worked so hard to get happy with."

Erica was right, and Jordan hated it nonetheless. So instead, they attempted to connect with Abigail repeatedly, bringing her her favorite teas, offering massages, and taking over in the kitchen for a while. They figured if they just did enough, she'd come back out of her shell. If Jordan could prove their love still existed in the midst of this darkness, Abbi would be happy again, right?

No. Nothing was working. No matter how hard they tried, no matter how much they did things differently, it wasn't bringing their Abbi Babbi sunshine back.

Imagining themselves in Abbi's shoes didn't help Jordan in the slightest with their desire to bargain for a better future. It only led to them feeling ill, dysphoric at the idea of bleeding out like that for up to a month. They already took pills that kept them from menstruating every month, allowing themselves to only have to endure it quarterly—and that was more than enough. They turned the idea of being pregnant over in their head and their stomach turned with violence. Erica was right. They weren't going to get pregnant, they didn't want Abbi trying again, and adopting during a pandemic was a big no.

Jordan went to the continuing Black Lives Matters demonstrations that were happening in Baltimore. Abigail, despite everything, did try to get out of bed for the one on June 10th. But, as she peeled a super-sized pad, coated thick with blood, and moved to replace it with another one, Jordan insisted without recourse that Abbi stay home. The last thing they both needed was Abbi collapsing on the streets in the middle of the summer's oppressive weather, bleeding out from the birth with nothing to show for it.

Abbi reflected her frustrations at being locked up in the house while Jordan fought for equality, recognition, and peace in a poem left in the Lesbian Book.

June 15th, 2020

Sweat, blood, and tears —
The cornerstones of hard work
And suffering alike.
One only needs to look to see
These glistening, telltale signs

Sticky on forehead, cheek, or thigh
To see my story.
Yet, is my grief worthy to be called such
When I am a little White girl, a femme,
Who can walk the streets without threat of a gun,
A chokehold,
A knee?
I can fear men, The Man, too,
But I cannot fear the color of my own skin.
I can fear my own body betraying me from within,
But my privilege plays out on the sidewalks.
Perhaps it is best this way; I clearly
Am no better than the Karens Who Cry Wolf
Over injustice that has nothing to do with justice.
This is all just the product of some larger code,
Patterns played out inside my rebellious body.
But what happens out there, the patterns of a
Patriarchal society. That is bigger. Much bigger,
And I beg you only to understand that I write
These words to try and work out my feelings,
Not because I think the sorrow of my few months
Is in any way equivalent to the sorrow of your entire
Bloodline. — Abbi

The poem seemed to speak to something even deeper Abbi must be grappling with. They were both in pain over the birth, but the rampaging racism eating away at their country definitely had a more profound impact on Jordan. They imagined Abbi must be trying to contend with her inability to show up fully for Jordan while everything was happening in their community and in their country. But, sitting down and having a long drawn-out talk about racism was not something Jordan had the mental resources to deal with at the moment, and it was even tiresome to have to try and carry Abbi's feelings in the midst of this fucked up shit, too.

With a creeping slowness, they were starting to realize it was not their job to deal with Abbi's feelings. Abbi could suffer all she needed to, but she also contributed to Jordan's suffering in ways they were now coming to terms with. Over the past two or so years, they'd tried to come out and say they couldn't stand Abbi's parents, that they were problematic, and that she shouldn't listen to a word they said. But, Jordan had never really pushed back, always trying to make sure Abbi felt supported in everything. The latest straw with Margie had perhaps been the most direct they'd ever gotten. Saying that had come with the disgusting realization that Abbi continuing to engage with her bigotted parents was passively accepting their worldview. That wasn't alright.

With little else to do but sink into despair if they thought too long, Jordan threw themself even more into work. The kids at the hospital needed them, still, and so that was where they would go. It was a place they felt safe and accepted. Their co-workers were understanding about their recent situation but also knew to give Jordan the space they needed. They started working overtime, making extra laps around the floor to check in on the kids. They brought toys and healthy snacks, colored with them, performed magic tricks, and even brought their guitar in to sing songs from popular kids shows. By the beginning of July, they had mastered some classics and new front-runners alike, such as the themes for Sesame Street, Daniel Tiger, Steven Universe, Peppa Pig, She-Ra, and Pete the Cat.

One of the patients Jordan visited often was a young girl of eight who had a slew of health complications: recurrent pneumonia with a variety of other respiratory issues, a compromised immune system, and physical anomalies in her lungs and throat. She was often found shaking and gasping for breath, coughing, and cold. Given everything going on with COVID-19, even those who had once visited her frequently were no longer allowed to in some cases, and certain members of the staff were spooked by the level of coughing.

Jordan didn't let that deter them.

"Hey Su-Su," they said, walking into the room the girl stayed in.

Susie looked up, blonde curls shaking. "Hi Jor-Jor."

Given her intense respiratory distress, Susie was always hooked up to an nasal cannula, a small tube with prongs in each nostril. When Jordan stopped by, they often practiced on the incentive spirometer, a device that taught her to use slow, deep breaths.

With the coronavirus continuing to cause anxiety for all, Jordan sat at a slightly more than social distance most days now while Susie did her breathing, and they opted to play games that didn't require physical contact—word association games, or sometimes even video games, each on a separate device.

"You look sadder than last time." Susie stopped her scribble on a page to study Jordan with her bright, curious eyes.

"Yeah? Well, I guess I need to play more jokes, then," Jordan said, standing up and fully preparing to ramp up the shenanigans.

"No." Susie waved a weak hand. Her voice was always so feeble when she spoke, like summoning the air was a challenge. "It's okay to be sad. You always tell me that. Were you lying?"

"Of course not, no." Jordan sat back down immediately, feeling chastised. "It is okay to be sad. I just—Don't want to cause you any worry, SuSu. It's time for fun, you know?"

The eight-year-old's gaze narrowed as she looked at Jordan. "Pretending your feelings aren't there doesn't work," she said, repeating something Jordan had taught her long ago. "It can just make them stronger because they'll do anything to get your attention."

Dammit, kids are good, Jordan reflected, bitter and amused.

"You're totally right, squiddo," they said. "Well, you're right then. I am sad."

"Why?"

"Well," this was where it got hard. If they opened up too much, they risked crossing ethical lines. If they clammed up, they demonstrated to this child that it was good to be guarded, even with someone you'd known a while. Perfecting the balance could be challenging. "My family is going through a very hard time right now."

"Because of the COVID stuff?"

"Yes, that's definitely a part of it," Jordan said, knowing it wasn't a lie. Being stuck in the house together so frequently while tension was high, not having good date nights out, being afraid of one of them getting sick, that was all woven in the tapestry of grief they faced together.

"What else?" Susie asked.

Jordan found themselves fiddling with the bottom hem of their work jacket, thumb stroking the stitching to soothe themselves. "Sometimes when adults are going through a hard time, they can say and do things they don't mean. As long as it doesn't happen in a neverending cycle, it's alright. It can just be a side effect of having something bad that's out of their control happen."

"What about if it keeps happening?"

"If it keeps happening, then sometimes those adults need to... Separate. Go their different ways. Not be together anymore."

"Is your wife going to not be with you anymore?"

"I don't know, Su-Su."

"That makes sense why you are sad then." Her child's cherub face screwed up with concentration for a moment as she struggled to breathe. She caught a breath after a moment and relaxed. "Remember, when it gets tough and your feelings are really really big, just put your hands on your belly and take a slow deep breath. Close your eyes, and picture your safe space."

Jordan almost couldn't believe this child listened so well to their advice.

"Do you go to your safe space a lot?" they asked.

"Mhm. There are castles made of candy there, and I have Barbies that guard me."

"That's pretty darn cool, Su-Su. Maybe I'll add some Barbies to mine."

"You should. They're pretty, and they're tall like you, and this one Barbie has..."

Jordan listened and didn't, all at once, smiling and nodding at the little girl as their own thoughts found themselves tumbling down new avenues, calling back up coping skills they'd let drift away in the midst of all the recent turmoil.

Their own internal safe space was the beach house where they'd stayed when they proposed to Abbi. That memory wasn't safe anymore. It hurt so, so much.

But, it'd all be alright. No matter what, it'd all be okay, and not because Abbi was smiling—but because Jordan was smiling. They looked up at Susie, strong and resilient, and they couldn't help but grin behind their mask. Susie could see it, too, probably in Jordan's eyes, and beamed a little smile back.

Abbi or no, they would not only get through this, but they'd be just fine. If they could embrace that fact, they could do absolutely anything.

DEPRESSION

Individuals may find themselves going through just one, or all, of the prior grief stages. However, they will finally approach the realization that the situation is real, allowing themselves time to grieve their loss.

Abigail

The house was quiet. Jordan seemed to be off in their own head or at work more often than they were home and present, and Abigail found herself doing her best to prepare for the return to school in just a few months' time. She was consistently distracted by the recent *everything* and fell further and further behind with each new sunrise.

Abbi's birthday came and went on July 8th, 2020. She wrote in the Lesbian Book that she didn't want Jory doing anything for her, and was very firm about it. This wasn't the time for any form of celebration. It was little over a month since Joscelin had passed on, COVID cases had skyrocketed with Florida now an epicenter for the pandemic, and civil unrest was spreading with good reason.

She found herself chewing through No. 2 pencil erasers and metal tips like mad, her mouth always needing something in it. Lately, she'd been eating everything she could get her fingers on, and the constant fugue state of gluten-fog was debilitating. She knew she needed to plan ahead for the upcoming school year, but it was an almost impossible feeling task. It didn't help that she felt guilty because Jor was still doing all the grocery shopping, and she was just consuming everything around her in an attempt to feel something—some shade of full that made sense. But, no matter how much she ate, she felt nothing but void.

Plan for smooth sailing; plan for success; plan for the course ahead; plan for the best.

A pencil end snapped between her teeth and she quickly spit it out, grabbing another one so that she could scribble the scraps of poems flowing through her.

She startled as her phone rang, rifling through papers on her desk to unbury the device. Erica's name appeared on the screen alongside a picture of her flashing a peace sign. It had been a while since they'd talked save a few text exchanges in which Abigail assured her she just needed space.

"Hi Erica," she said, feeling a pang of regret upon seeing Erica's worried face.

"Finally." Erica teared up. "How ya doing, Abs?"

Abigail picked up another pencil and began chewing at the metal bit. She paused long enough to say, "About like this."

Erica and Abigail had gone to school together from 6th grade on. Erica knew perhaps better than anyone that chewing pencil ends meant Abigail was stressed beyond tolerance.

"I figured as much. It's good to see you, again," Erica said.

Abigail nodded. "Yeah. It's good to see you, too. I'm sorry we haven't been able to see each other recently and that I've not been in the space to talk. Honestly, I'm just feeling really depressed now."

"That's pretty understandable. How is Jor?"

"I don't know. I feel like I can't look at them lately. I feel... I feel so much guilt because I can't take away their pain of being Black in America, and I'm over here just being this completely self-consumed White woman. Like... God, I am a complete bitch. I should be able to just pull all my emotions in and take care of Jor through this, but all I can seem to do is eat, sleep, and cry. I don't even know if I should be married to them anymore, honestly."

Erica frowned. Abigail watched her start braiding her hair to the side, her own nervous tick.

While fumbling with the braid, Erica said, "Jor loves you. I know you love Jor, too. It's reasonable to be depressed like I said, but the marriage bit comes down to you. You choose to stay married or not. You choose how you engage in the relationship. How much you open up. Your relationship has never faced a challenge like this before... Corona, systemic racism, the loss of a child, the tension of your parents' opinions... It's a lot."

"And I don't know if our relationship is strong enough to endure it all. I don't know if I am strong enough."

"Sounds like you need some soul searching, Abs. Like, hardcore."

"I think you're right." She bit down on her pencil again, enjoying the grind of the metal against her teeth. "Not being able to get out of this house just gives me no space to really think. Yeah, I can walk around downtown, but everything being closed or only partially accessible ruins it. I can't even get comfort from all the things I'd normally love. I can't get a cupcake from that one window shop. I can't go touch all the books at Atomic. I can't play with the mushrooms on the table at foraged. I can't go sit in the psychic shop and bolt at the last second like I always do because I chicken out. I can't visit you. I can't visit my parents, and I don't know if I want to... Wait, Erica, what do you mean about the tension of my parents?"

Erica gave Abigail a look that made her blood feel like car coolant, racing through her veins with a chill that ricocheted of every vertebra.

"Please tell me you didn't just ask that question."

"I... Did," Abigail said.

"Never ask Jordan that question, I swear. Are you completely blind to what your parents do? What they say? Hell, at the New Years party alone, your mom had to forcibly quell probably ten seriously racist statements. You can't willfully ignore their bigotry forever if you want to be a good partner to Jordan."

It stung unbelievably. Abigail's internal landscape shifted from shame to guilt to anger back to shame. She was speechless, so Erica continued after a pause.

"Soul searching is mandatory, stat. I'll see what I can do to figure out an escape so you can get some peace of mind away from the house. Hang tight, Abs. Love you. But, don't be a dumbass, okay?"

Over the following weeks, Abigail tried to overcome her thoughts and connect with Jordan. But, it felt too overwhelming. The very act of reaching out for her partner made flashbacks of the hospital surge. There were flickers of their night in the bedroom when she'd gotten pregnant that rather than being intimate and loving were now the object of horror and loss. She felt crushed by the shame of everything. When she wasn't feeling overwhelmed by the void inside her, she was spaced out and floating, staring at nothing in particular.

Black and blue. Red and white. Color means everything, symbolism in paint. She scratched a line through the words, dragging it slowly backward from the t all the way to the B. Poems were harder now, too, while drowned in her depression. Life felt like there was a wet, weighted blanket on top of her. Breathing was about all she had the energy for, and sometimes not even that. But, she had to write these lessons, had to find the right words within her to reveal her most unburied feelings, and had to come back to life. She had to do something different or she really would have nothing left to show for the last three years, let alone few months.

July 25th, 2020

I'D DO JUST ABOUT ANYTHING FOR YOU, ABBI. JUST ABOUT ANYTHING. WHAT I WON'T DO IS GIVE MYSELF UP. I'VE DONE THAT FOR A WHILE, I'M STARTING TO REALIZE. I'VE SPENT SO LONG GETTING LOST IN YOUR SMILES THAT I REACHED A POINT WHERE I'D SACRIFICE MY OWN SANITY FOR YOUR SAKE. BUT, I CAN'T DO THAT

ANYMORE. IT'S NOT GOOD FOR YOU, AND IT'S NOT GOOD FOR ME.

I'VE REALIZED HERE LATELY THAT I'VE GIVEN INTO YOU OVER AND OVER ON LITTLE THINGS, AND NOW A BIG THING, BECAUSE I DIDN'T WANT TO BE LIKE YOUR FAMILY WHO NEVER SUPPORTED YOU. I WANTED TO BE THE ULTIMATE SUPPORT. BUT, THERE IS A HEALTHY LEVEL OF THAT, AND THEN THERE IS... THIS.

WHEN WE GOT MARRIED, WE AGREED TO ENDURE THE HARD TIMES. I DON'T EVEN FEEL LIKE YOU'RE TRYING ANYMORE. I GUESS WHEN I PICTURED US ENDURING SOME SORT OF LOSS, I PICTURED US HOLDING EACH OTHER. MAYBE LIKE WE DID IN THE BEGINNING OF THE CORONA THING WHEN IT ALL JUST SEEMED LIKE A BOOGEYMAN. BUT, I DO UNDERSTAND THAT ENDURING THIS, A MAJOR GLOBAL TRAUMA, ON TOP OF AMERICA BEING A RACIST PILE OF SHIT, ON TOP OF YOUR CAREER GETTING DISRUPTED, US LOSING OUR CHILD... IT'S A LOT FOR ANYONE.

BUT, I'M NOT GOING TO SIT HERE AND PRETEND I CAN GO AT IT LIKE THIS FOREVER. I MISS OUR TOUCHES, OUR KISSES, OUR JOKES. I MISS THE WAY WE FINISH EACH OTHER'S SENTENCES. IT'S BEEN ABOUT FOUR MONTHS NOW SINCE THIS NIGHTMARE BEGAN, AND I SAID THE SAME BACK THEN. I DON'T KNOW WHAT YOU NEED TO DO, BUT PLEASE DO IT. SCREAM AT THE TOP OF YOUR LUNGS. BREAK SOME DISHES. GET THERAPY. LEAVE ME. BUT, WHATEVER YOU NEED TO DO, PLEASE DO IT SOON. I DESERVE A PARTNER, NOT A GHOST. I'M NOT SHAMING YOU FOR HAVING A ROUGH TIME WITH THIS, BUT IF YOU CAN'T LET ME IN, CAN'T EVEN LET ME HOLD

YOU, LET'S STOP EXISTING IN THIS HOLLOW SHELL OF A
RELATIONSHIP.

TO BE IN A RELATIONSHIP, IT REQUIRES WE HAVE
SOME FORM OF RELATING. THE ONLY THING REMOTELY
RELATING ABOUT OUR SITUATION NOW IS BEING IN
THIS HOUSE TOGETHER. IT'S NOT ENOUGH TO MAKE A
MARRIAGE. I DON'T WANT TO LIVE A LIFE WHERE I CAN
ONLY BE WITH YOU IN MY HEAD AND HEART.

THINK ABOUT IT. I RESPECT WHATEVER YOU NEED IN THE
END, BUT I ALSO RESPECT MYSELF ENOUGH TO CHOOSE
ACTIONS THAT FOLLOW THROUGH ON WHAT I NEED, TOO.

WITH LOVE, —JORY

When Abigail closed the notebook, placing it on the
counter to indicate it had been read, her hands were willow
branches in the wind. It felt like her body might betray her
again—she might buckle and not get back up. The only
thing that saved her was a timely call from Erica. Shaking,
she answered.

"Hey."

"Hey." Erica didn't bother with formalities but
launched right into why she had called. "I think I've found
you an opportunity to get away. The shelter's owner says
she has a brother who does AirBnB rentals. He hasn't had
his properties open though due to COVID. But, she asked

him if he'd make an exception for a friend of a friend and he said he would, so long as it was just going to be used by one person and you had no symptoms."

"That would be... Real good." Abigail heard her own disembodied voice jittering in her throat just as much as her hands trembled on the phone.

"You doing alright over here?"

Abigail was so glad that she couldn't see Erica for once. She knew seeing her face would undo her right now. "I'm alright. Just read a new entry by Jory in the Book."

"Ah. A doozy?"

"Yeah. I think we might be getting a divorce after all," Abigail said.

There was a crackle of static on the other end a moment before Erica spoke again. "You'll get through this, Abs. For now, how about we just get you set up to travel? The property is in New Jersey, probably about three hours from your house. It's near the water. I know that's quite a hike, but you might appreciate the drive and the sights along the way."

"That sounds perfect."

"I thought it might. You could rent something local, but I know the feels when you just want to get up and go far away. He said you can go anytime after August 8th due to the weather warnings coming up."

"I don't know if I can survive that long, Erica."

A sigh. "Let me see what I can do."

About three hours later, Erica called back to report that she'd managed to bump it up to August 1st. Abigail could stay as long as she needed to.

Six days was a better turnaround than close to two weeks, so she bit her tongue, thanked Erica, and wrote down the details in the back of her poetry book.

The Friday before she was set to leave, Abigail asked Jory if they'd like to have a date night. The look of Jordan's face was confused, at best, eyebrows furrowed, head tilted.

"Tonight?"

"Yeah, tonight."

"What will we do?"

"I don't know, a movie, maybe. Netflix?" Abigail tried on a smile. She could feel the way her lips and cheeks resisted, drawing back down like tiny metal weights were pulling them back into place.

Jordan, tone skeptical, said, "Yeah, sure."

The ambivalence about broke Abigail in two again. They'd meant what they wrote in the notebook. They were really on the closer side of done, and Abigail had driven them to that point.

They agreed to watch Stardust, a movie Abigail had watched when she was younger and loved, but Jory had never seen. Abigail offered a hand to Jordan who took it as soon as the movie turned on, and immediately regretted her choice. Jory's hand in hers made her think of the hospital. She found it hard to breathe but focused her attention on the screen.

The message was far too appropriate for their situation, despite the fantasy elements. Seeing a baby in the film made her wince, but beyond that, the whole theme was about love overcoming darkness—literally. Love was the force that ended the evil forces at play. Abigail tried not to cry, but failed spectacularly as she looked over to find Jordan crying, too.

After the movie was over, they ordered takeout from one of the Chinese places off the Avenue, and sat eating lo mein and spring rolls at the table. Abigail could feel the weight of knowing she was going away tomorrow, maybe for good. Despite the "niceness" of the evening, she still felt completely detached from Jor, like she was looking at a stranger. She didn't like it at all, but it was her present reality.

"I can see why you like that movie," Jor said at the table. "Yeah, it's good."

"I really appreciated the symbolism," Jordan added. "The wall, especially. I could see the wall being a metaphor for so many things."

These were the sorts of conversations Abigail once lived for. She taught literature. She breathed poetry. But, she just didn't have the energy for deep talks with Jordan. Jordan, yet again, was putting in the effort she just couldn't seem to manage.

"Jory? Why do you still bother with me?"

Jordan set their chopsticks down, sucking up the last bite of their noodles. "What do you mean?"

"Why are you still with me after all this? I've been the world's biggest asshole."

She watched Jordan push away the takeout container, instead folding their hands together on the table.

"I know how good you can be. And, I may or may not have a professional level of knowledge about trauma. I want you to be well, but I can't make you get well. I've been trying to give you that space, you know?"

"That doesn't really answer the question."

"I guess it doesn't. It's because I love you. The real you. Your true self. You're not in your true self anymore. You're all hijacked by emotions, which I do understand, I promise... But, being perfectly blunt, I am starting to wonder if I got a bad read on your true self. I just can't wrap my head around certain choices you make. Why you go about things the way you do. I don't get your attachment to your mom, for example. It's... trauma bonding. There is nothing good there."

Abigail found herself wanting to defend her mother as soon as those words left Jor's mouth, but instead, she anchored into her conversation with Erica. She had been absolutely blind around Jordan's feelings. Erica was completely right.

"I... I hope you got my true self, right, too, Jory."

After dinner, they parted ways, Abigail returning to her office with the Lesbian Book and Jordan to the new music room which they'd been cobbling together. It was once going to be the baby's room, but that obviously wasn't needed anymore.

At her desk, Abigail chewed on her pencil and tapped her foot nervously as she stared down at the page. She'd be leaving early tomorrow morning before Jory was likely to get up. Jor never liked to get up early on Saturdays. So, she'd write her farewell in the notebook tonight, then sneak her bags out to the car.

She could hear Jordan strumming on the guitar in the other room, their soulful, bluesy voice practicing a new song they were writing based on Animal Crossing. A lot of the kids at the hospital were obsessed even months after the initial hype of the new Switch game.

Dragging the pencil tip lightly down the side of the notebook, Abigail contemplated how to approach this entry. A letter? A poem? Both? What did she really want to say? What could possibly convey the depth of things even she didn't know?

Sucking in a breath, she opened to a fresh page, put the pencil down, and let it flow. Only when her tears hit the page did she realize she was crying again.

FIGHT OR FLIGHT

*A physiological reaction in response to stress.
Changes are caused by the activation of the
sympathetic nervous system by adrenaline,
which prepares the body to challenge or flee
from a perceived threat.*

JORDAN

When you've been attached to someone for so long, you
can feel their absence profoundly.

Jordan realized this as they sat up in bed Saturday
afternoon. The house was dead. There was no Abbi
scratching away at a notebook or cooking. No sound of
the TV on. Just nothingness. Dread settled into their
stomach, a sinking ship plummeting to the bottom.

Throwing on a house robe and slippers, Jordan ran
downstairs hoping the worst had not happened and that
Abbi had just gone out somewhere.

They headed right for the window where the Lesbian
Book sat expectedly. Relief swelled from their toes to their

head as they realized there was at least some explanation for this silent, still morning.

August 1st, 2020

The Hero is no Hero;
but she approaches the innermost cave anyway.
Danger lurks, but she knows she must face her fears and go deep,
Deep
into the ground.
Is the grail somewhere in there? Is it buried treasure
or right beneath her fingertips at the mouth?
To find out she must descend into hell, for only there
can she find what she must face. Will she rescue a princess,
slay a dragon, or bring something back from the dead?
I've been less than good to you. To me. To the world. To the memory
of it all. I don't know what I'm doing, but I'm going to try and
figure it out. I know on the other end of this, there are really only
two choices. Or at least, that's what I can imagine. Maybe I'll find
something else while I'm gone. Maybe I'll find myself.
Please don't worry about me. Erica knows where I am and we'll be
in touch in case of anything. I want you to take this time to do things
you enjoy. Blast music. Dance around naked. Experience what life
without a wet rag can be like. You deserve that.

When I come back, we'll figure out where to go from here. I know last night was awkward. I'm sorry for that. I don't know what I'm doing right now, but you deserve a partner who does. She might be me, or she might be someone else. Time will tell, but I know there isn't too much time left.

I'll always love you, even if I don't show it. — Abbi

Jordan allowed the sense of loneliness to sink in as they shut the book and put in on the counter. An only child, they'd struggled with loneliness when they were young. They'd struggled, too, with all the visits to the hospital. Dad and Mom were that couple always attached at the hip, so when Mom got sick, Dad spent a majority of his time at her side rather than working or tending to Jordan. They'd adjusted quickly to the hospital setting, and it was a social worker there that had really helped them get through the alienation and isolation. Jordan could name every corridor at the hospital—could probably draw a map of the place, even now.

Abbi had left muffins on the counter. Jordan selected one, then walked out back with a cup of coffee. It was a hot and sunny day, right up to the edge of unbearably muggy. Sinking into one of the porch chairs, they allowed their body to stretch out like a cat trying to sit like a human, legs wide, back curved. The mug sat on their belly, one hand gingerly keeping it in place.

Their mother, Tonya, had been a lot like Abbi from what they could remember. Well, the Abbi of old. Wide-eyed with wonder, artistic, soft of body, but loud in spirit and volume. Mom was a force to be reckoned with, and Jordan recalled Mom trying to argue with Dad about spending more time with their child versus her all the time. But, he just couldn't seem to give up the gig of Mom's sidekick.

It had left Jordan feeling "less than" far more times than was acceptable, just like Abbi withdrawing. Despite how much energy Jordan put in, Abbi had been a wall just like Dad. Jordan tried so hard to be seen. To be heard. But, it didn't make any difference when the ones you loved were wrapped up in their own heads. They couldn't blame Abbi, and yet they could. They didn't want to blame her, though. That wasn't what this was about. This was about acknowledging the fucked up nature of it all. Twenty twenty could eat an entire bag full of dicks, for all Jordan cared at this point.

They wondered where Abbi was going. What would she find in the innermost cave of her hero's journey? Despite the anguish of the last months, of finding the poem, Jordan couldn't help but smirk at how even now as they grappled with chaos and potential divorce, Abbi was still thinking like the passionate English scholar she was. But, this whole thing had been a bit of a hero's journey. They stared up at the clouds, trying to remember each of the steps. A call to adventure, crossing the threshold, tests, allies, and enemies. There were certainly some aspects of real life that were like a story. Now, all that was left to be determined was whether the hero or in this case, Abbi, would survive the ordeal at the end and defeat the darkness inside her. Jordan just hoped there was no danger-filled road back.

Abigail

Bright green pastures. Waterside views. Grey paved roads and skylines. The world turns. Life goes on. No matter how much I might try to ignore the call, it is there. It is all right there.

Abigail wished she'd realized sooner how powerful just getting in a car and driving could be. It felt freeing to be on the road. Yes, she had a destination, but the journey there was so, so good. She found herself marveling at the late summer growth sprouting up along the roads, the trees still vibrant and full of life before fall. Life existed all around her, and it was good to see that again.

Life. Death. She had experienced both in her own body now. The moment that child's brain and skull had failed to develop properly, life had transitioned to death right inside her womb. Would she now allow the rest of her life to die? It was still uncertain.

She'd been taught from a young age that a woman's job was to create. To give birth. For her entire now 33 years on Earth, she had experienced nonstop pressure to bear children. Even on this drive, she had passed a fertility billboard targeted toward cis women and their biological clocks. It had made her feel ill. Was that all women were good for? Procreation? Making sandwiches in the kitchen? Following her husband's wise orders? Certainly, a good deal of society thought this way, and perhaps she had let herself think this way wrongly, too.

As the road curved and wound, she remembered a road trip her family had once had taken. Dad was driving. Mom was in the front seat. Her and her brother Jack were in the back. She must have been 6; Jack would have been about 16. They were going to a beach in Delaware, driving in from Pennsylvania where they'd lived.

"I'm so proud of you, son," Dad said. "You're going to make a fine soldier. I couldn't be happier."

Jack had just decided officially to enlist the following year. Abigail couldn't grasp what that really meant.

"It's sad little Abigail will never be so much use to this country, but she can certainly raise children that will. Perhaps another in the line to raise through the ranks." Dad slapped his knee.

Abigail didn't register what it really meant, but she'd known from the way Jack sneered at her and the way Mom's hands rubbed together that it wasn't good.

"Can't I be a soldier, too?" Abigail asked, confused.

Her dad and Jack discharged such a rapid-fire of laughter, she felt the wound immediately.

"You're weak and fat, Abigail," Jack said. "And girls don't belong in the military. When you're older, all those hormones are going to take over and you'll never be able to keep a level head."

"Damn right. Girls are just ticking time bombs waiting to go off. No place in the ranks for that."

Mom, trying to repair it, turned around to look at Abigail. "It's okay, honey. You're going to make a lovely mother and housewife. You could maybe even go to college and get a degree in something. Maybe be a school teacher. That'd be really nice. I'll make sure you can have a career, too, if you'd like that."

And, she'd been good for her word on that. When Abigail turned 16, Mom had explained she could apply to any school she'd like. As it turned out, Mom had used her "allowance" from Dad over the years to create a college fund.

Her grip on the steering wheel brought her back to the present. It hurt to see with such clarity how her upbringing had impacted her. Had she managed to avoid anything at all about her parent's brainwashing? She was a good teacher, but was that really what she wanted to do? Did she really want kids? What did she want? Jory had been the only independent choice she'd ever made, and she'd made it the second she laid eyes on them in that classroom all those years ago. It had been the biggest, most radical thing she'd ever done, and she wasn't sure presently whether she regretted it or not.

Jordan

Jordan strummed on their guitar, sitting out back again. There was a relatively nice breeze that stirred pleasantly through their hair. It had grown out nicely, and they actually found themselves admiring their reflection as they teased the onyx curls to give them more volume. Sure, having the sides shaved was nice, but this was, too. The wind reminded them of the way Abbi's fingers often felt on the back of their neck, and they sighed. Why did it always seem to go back to her?

Who was Jordan without Abbi? They'd had that breakthrough at work so recently about their independence and how they'd be okay without her, but now that she was gone, were they really okay?

Fingers plucking at strings, they remembered one of their last conversations with their Mom. They hadn't realized she was about to die, not really, but they'd felt it was a good time to tell her they might not be a girl.

"Mom, I don't think I'm a girl."

"Alright. What are you?"

"I don't know," Jordan had said. "I don't feel like a boy or a girl."

"There could be something in between, or neither at all," Mom had said, completely open to the conversation. "I tell you what, when you're older, read some good books. Toni Morrison might be a place to start. Maybe it'll give you some ideas."

Jordan had listened. They'd read everything by Toni Morrison they could uncover. Also Maya Angelou. Octavia Butler. These Black women questioned so much. They questioned White Patriarchal America. They questioned gender norms. They pushed for Black voices to take the literary world by force, and they succeeded in elevating themselves in a way that inspired Jordan with every page turned.

It wasn't until quite recently that they'd discovered the term nonbinary. Like many nonbinary folx, Jordan had been left without a word for a long time—had felt the need to transition to be a trans man if they wanted to be acknowledged as anything other than a woman. But, they'd quickly realized after a short stint on T that it wasn't what they wanted either. When at last they intersected the liminal spaces of gender, they'd found peace that permeated every queer cell of their body.

The fight for their identity hadn't ended there, naturally. People questioned why they didn't transition fully. Why they got top surgery if they weren't actually a man. How they could call themselves a lesbian if they weren't actually a woman. There were plenty of people who tried to police their identity, and it was like hearing music for the first time when Abbi had come along and respected their words right away.

"The denotation of words," she'd said, "is pretty well agreed on due to those words being recorded in dictionaries, but the connotations or emotional implications vary from person to person. What matters most is how the words feel for you personally. If you're happy, so am I. Use the labels you love." She'd smiled, squeezed Jordan's wrist, and jaunted off to grab them both another coffee from the café.

The only time Abbi had ever called any aspect of their identity into question was when she claimed Jordan wasn't a real parent. That was the worst thing Abbi had ever said, really, and Jordan wouldn't have been able to forgive her if they weren't so familiar with how the human mind worked. As she'd said in her note, though, time would tell whether or not she came back around and this wreck could be salvaged.

Abigail

She arrived in good time to the property. It was a quick walk to the beach at only about five blocks. The property was a cute little house with bushes out front, bay windows, and a fenced-in yard. After unpacking, she opted to walk down to the bay area where she was shocked to find it crowded despite being mid-pandemic. She supposed people in the world were getting antsy about restrictions—she was, too.

Jor and her had taken a trip to the beach only once so far in their relationship. It was a few months before their nuptials on summer break—in fact it was when they got engaged. They hadn't even moved to Hampden yet.

Jory had written her a song and played it on the beach in front of onlookers, then dropped to one knee after the ballad was done to offer Abbi a rainbow ring. Abbi had sobbed. Jory had grinned, then sobbed, too. The song was beautiful, though all she could remember of the lyrics were the chorus: "*So if I should live another day, don't let it be without you. The brightest light I've ever seen, you've given me a clear view; let it be, oh let it be, that you feel the same as I do.*"

She wondered if they'd ever take a beach trip again, and found herself not wanting to stay there alone. After only about twenty minutes in the sand and sun, she went back to the house.

The back area of the house was unique and beautiful. There were large planters with wildflowers, an umbrella table, and some outdoor benches. There was no fire pit or grill, but there was a small cobblestone walkway to the back of the fence and gate. Abigail ordered delivery from a nearby pizza place, then gorged herself on an entire Neapolitan while she tapped her pencil against her poetry book.

She napped, ate, napped, scribbled. Paced. Screamed. Napped again. She slept all the way through the night and well into the next morning, feeling rather out of sorts. Inside. Outside. Inside. Outside. It was nice in the backyard, so she opted to sit out there much of the time, reminiscing.

Why had her relationship with Jordan taken such a hit lately? Her, of course. Jordan had tried to show up time and time again in the beginning of this nightmare, but she just couldn't take the affection. There was a pervasive sense that she was being punished, she realized, and she had perpetuated it by not allowing her partner in.

Abigail remembered when she came out around her twenty-third birthday. She was doing a five-year Masters program, but she'd applied herself so much, she'd actually be finishing after the upcoming fall semester. When she announced to her family and friends on Facebook that she was queer, her mother had called her in tears saying that her father said she couldn't come to Thanksgiving or Christmas that year. They also didn't attend her college graduation, something she had worked so hard to obtain. Dad, she understood, but Mom... Why hadn't Mom come? After all, it was thanks to her that Abigail had gone to school and not had to pay a single cent.

Sometime the next year, after an appropriate amount of time "grieving," they invited her to Easter. Things had been tense, and Jack and his wife attended with their young son, Liam. Jack pulled Abigail aside and told her she was never to bring a woman around Liam and indicate she was gay. If she ever brought a girlfriend home, she'd need to say it was just a friend.

Abigail hadn't known what to think, but she still wanted to have a good relationship with her mother. It was something she was desperate for.

"I am so proud of you for graduating college," Mom offered, giving her a hug. But, she said it quietly in a way that indicated Dad shouldn't overhear such an admission.

When Abigail had met Jordan a few years ago and excitedly called Mom to tell her about them, Mom was at first excited, then confused by the use of pronouns.

"Are you dating multiple people? That's unacceptable," she'd said.

"N—no?" Abigail actually hadn't known what to say because she sort of had a thing with Erica who had come out as pansexual recently, and despite being in a long term relationship with Alex, had a few other relationships, too. But could they classify themselves as in a relationship? It wasn't the same as it was with Jordan, but she wouldn't give Erica up for anything, either.

She'd tried to explain nonbinary to her mother who had affirmed Jordan was just "confused" and hoped "she" would decide to be a "man" instead. One point for kind of, sort of, being maybe okay with trans people? No, she couldn't even give Mom that.

Mom and Dad's first meeting with Jordan had gone quite poorly. Well, after the fact. They had somehow managed to put on a strong face upon meeting them, but when Mom called Abigail later and said, "You didn't tell us she was Black," Abigail thought the world might end. Jordan was standing right there and overheard, and it led to the first argument of their relationship.

"I didn't think it would matter?" Abigail had said as Jordan stormed out of the room.

But, it mattered to her parents. And, in truth, it mattered to Abigail, too, but not for the same reasons. Being Black gave Jordan a different view on the world. She'd never understand what it meant to be nonbinary or Black, but she understood what it meant to be queer, to be different, and to experience rejection, even if nowhere on the same scale. It mattered that Jordan's experiences were uniquely theirs. And it mattered, now, that Abigail was leaving Jordan behind.

This was no way to be a wife. It was no way to be an ally. It was no way to be.

JORDAN

On the third day Abbi was gone, Jordan started to accept that when she came back, it might be to tell them she wanted a divorce. It was a hard thing to swallow, but they did their best to call up the feeling they'd had after talking to their client Susie. Their worth wasn't determined by another person. They didn't need to rely on Abigail to be happy. And they certainly didn't need to let people that excused opinions that were anti-them to be in their life if that was the choice they willingly made. That was a realization that packed a gut punch with it.

Their mom would have been 100% pro-Abbi, as long as Abbi was 100% pro-Jordan. Was she though? Jordan chewed their lip, strumming away absently, as they thought about all the times they hadn't spoken up for themself when Abbi was around her parents. They shouldn't have to defend themself in that way though. It was a complex battle—who was in the right or wrong here? Was anyone? Abbi desperately wanted her mother's love, and Jordan was able to understand how much Abbi's mom had done for her, especially financially.

But, was the love of a mother who could only love you half way really worth it? They couldn't imagine it was. They realized that they'd feared speaking their truth to Abbi for worry she would abandon them; perhaps Abbi feared speaking up to her mom more openly because she was worried about losing her, too. It was the same. It was different. It was so exhausting to think about.

Jordan opted to explore new music. It was something that always took their mind off things. They started digging down a YouTube rabbit hole of acoustic unplugged interviews, holding their guitar as they leaned back in their computer chair. Each song lived out an entire lifetime in lyrics, stirring Jordan's imagination.

They began searching symbolism for grief and loss, finding everything from certain colors or roses to magpies and cypress trees.

The world shifted as their own lyrics began to form in their mind, drawing upon the chorus of the song they'd written as a proposal to Abigail. That moment had been perfect. It had been everything.

Jordan's heart plucked as they began to pick at the strings on their guitar. They tried a few words, singing low.

"I'm holding on to something new, something old, and something blue.

I'm holding on to white balloons that carry all my sorrow.

Her spark of life, now that it's gone, was something that we borrowed.

Let us learn, and let us grow, from all she wanted us to know.

Is this life, or is this pain? Let this wash away with rain...

If I should live another day, don't let it be without you.

You're the brightest light I've ever seen, you've given me a clear view;

let it be, oh let it be, you feel the same as I do.

No matter what we've been through,
No matter what we've been through."

Abigail

The sky was dreary and cloudy the morning of the third full day there. She got up early to make coffee and sit out back, only this time, she was holding something she'd brought along with her: a divorce contract. She'd printed it off before she'd left, determined to sit and really think over what Jor had said. She knew that Jory deserved the world and she wasn't providing that at this point.

Truth was, Abigail didn't know how to talk about her feelings. She knew how to talk about literature. She knew how to teach. Hell, she knew how to be loud and proud, but never how to speak up against her parents or expose the core of her emotions to someone. Whenever she'd tried that as a kid, it had ended in Mom and Dad fighting, Jack ridiculing her, being grounded, told not to cry, or any other manner of unpleasant things. Mom always tried to defend her, but it was never quite enough. Abigail would never be able to understand why she stayed with Dad, just like she couldn't understand now why Jor was staying with her.

Jor hated being alone. Jor liked talking about feelings. Jor was a beautiful person with a heart of pure unicorn and fairy dust—magical. And Abigail was giving them a mere shadow of what she could be.

Abbi held the divorce papers for a moment more, then set it down on the glass tabletop in front of her. The umbrella kept her cool despite the summer's scorch. She stared at it for a long moment, then shifted her gaze to her phone. It was tempting to call Jordan, but she couldn't bring herself to do that quite yet, either. There was a battle being pitched out inside of her, and she wasn't ready to pull Jory into it.

Instead, she picked up the phone to call Mom.

Margie picked up on the third ring. "Hey sweetie. How are you?"

"I'm... I don't know, Mom. I'm in New Jersey. I had to get out of the house."

"Trouble in paradise?" Mom asked, and she sounded actually concerned.

"I guess so—I've just been cooped up in that house for so long. I was bleeding during all the local protests, so I couldn't even get out there to participate in those, and I just feel like I'm not showing up for Jor at all."

She heard her mother's sharp inhale. "You wouldn't really consider going and participating in all those riots, would you? People smashing things and looting things? It's criminal, Abigail."

"The protests have been almost completely peaceful, Mom."

"Not from what I've seen. If these Black people would just realize that they already have equality and—"

"What? Mom, what are you saying?"

"I just can't get behind this whole Black Lives Matter thing. Of course they do. All lives matter. Anyone who thinks their life is somehow more special than others is just ridiculous. Please tell me Jordan isn't one of them."

Abigail was stunned. Was it this obvious the whole time?

"Mom, that's not at all what Black Lives Matter is about. They don't think they're superior in any way. They're targeted constantly by systemic oppression and police—"

"You know, your little nephew Liam is thinking of entering the police force. You shouldn't talk about police officers like that. And your father's best friend—"

"Mom—"

"Anyway, that's rather unpleasant talk. Tell me, have you decided when you'll try again for another baby?"

Abigail swallowed. Felt shivers race from belly to shoulders and ripple down her arms. Nausea. Anger. Sadness.

"No. To be honest with you Mom, I'm not sure I want kids. I thought I did and when you mentioned wishing for it for Christmas, I... I don't know what got into me, but I just gave in."

"Nonsense. You've wanted kids your whole life. Remember you and your baby dolls? You always carried them around everywhere."

"Because you told me I was going to be a mother when I grew up. Because Dad wouldn't let me play with anything else."

"That's not true!" Margie sounded scolded. "You always gravitated toward them in the store."

"Because that's what I was trained to do, Mom!"

Margie gasped. "Abigail Rose Miller, what are you on about right now? Coming out as gay, marrying outside your race and religion. I think you going to a Liberal Arts school was your father and my downfall. They fed you so much nonsense there..."

Abigail couldn't even hear her mother anymore. She'd spotted something moving in the bushes and squinted. She heard the buzzing before she made the shapes out.

"I've got to go, Mom."

Abigail hung up the phone and stood, moving slowly toward the bush. The energy of the space felt somehow different rather suddenly, and the sky had a yellow overcast to it. Her nerves flared, and a sense of imminent doom alongside intense hope swelled in her chest.

JORDAN

Jordan couldn't sleep, so instead, they sat in the music room opening their mouth to sing. They'd spent enough hours now playing chords on repeat and testing lyrics that the song they were developing had become an anthem. A lifeline. They hoped wherever Abbi was, she could hear their heart singing.

"Even when life batters us, this raging, waring storm, our white balloons will carry us home, and safe, and warm.

It might seem too impossible, you might think we will end,

but I'm sending my love on the wind and promise not to bend.

Is this life, or is this pain? Let this wash away with rain..."

Abigail

Abigail neared the bush. There was a tumult of movement, a dramatic shake, and then a swarm of bees burst forth, sending her stumbling back. She fell on the sidewalk, the breath knocked from her with force. Above her, the bees surged into the air, dancing, swirling, making her dizzy.

She'd never felt such extreme emotion, not even in the worst moments of the past few months. And this... This was absolute joy. Absolute, all in, overflowing love.

She remembered the bumble bee ornament, the bees buzzing outside when she was pregnant, the ones that had graced the clovers in the backyard at home. The faint sound of buzzing in the atmosphere penetrated through the worst parts of it all. It made sense. It was a whisper. An earful from Joscelin who had been the symbol of Jory's love for Abigail. Jory's neverending willingness to show up for her. Jory's constant support, validation, concern, and adoration.

In this moment, it was like Joscelin was right there. Like all the love in the world a child could give a parent was being compacted into Abigail's body all at once. It was like the bees were waving at her, little yellow and black messengers from the beyond.

You have all the love you need, they seemed to be saying. *Don't settle for less than absolute respect.*

She found herself sobbing, hyperventilating, staring up at the cloud of bees that lingered far longer than made sense.

JORDAN

"Is this life, or is this pain? Let this wash away with rain.

Despair has shackled us in shame, but now we must break free..."

Jordan found themself crying as they sang the words. Abbi had been through a hard time, and so had they. They were both changing. Would it bring them together, or cast them apart?

Abigail

As she lay sprawled on the ground, her elbows propping her up, a memory surfaced. It was about a month into her relationship with Jory. They were talking about their future already having moved in together, and the baby buzz had hit hard.

"As fun as it is to think about kids," Jor had explained, "A lot of this is just hormonal. Evolutionarily, it's perfectly normal for people to get swept up in each other early on and want to have kids because the hormones our bodies fill with are meant to encourage reproduction. That's how we've survived as a species. Ever wondered why most relationships don't make it much past a year or two?"

It had been a shocking revelation to Abigail, but once it settled in, she'd been able to laugh about it. The two of them agreed they didn't really want kids because they wanted to travel a bunch when they were still young, and besides, Darrel was far away and her Catholic parents couldn't be trusted with any children they had. They'd be the grandparents that tried converting children to Catholicism forcefully, and urge them not to be gay, as if such a thing were a choice.

On top of that, Abigail really wanted to write books, become a motivational speaker that traveled around the world, and speak up against injustice. Jor wanted to be able to volunteer with other people's kids and maybe open a music center for underprivileged children. They both already put so much work into children, and they had much more energy to give without having any of their own.

Abigail shook her head, clearing the fog that had settled in on her. *Of all the lousy realizations about yourself to have,* she thought, *the realization of how brainwashed you've been has got to be the worst.*

JORDAN

"Despair has shackled us in shame, but now we must break free..."

Jordan sang, belting this line in particular. It was their vow that if Abbi came home and wanted to work things out, they would never be quiet again. They wouldn't let her get away with giving in to her mother's pressure, no matter the reason. They wouldn't let her make choices on a whim. They'd support her in getting the help she needed to get through everything.

"If I should live another day, don't let it be without you.

You're the brightest light I've ever seen, yet I can see right through you."

Abigail

"Who am I?" Abigail whispered to herself. Then, louder. "Who am I?"

The bees flew away as a nasty-looking storm cloud blew into view overhead. Still stunned by the whole experience, Abigail pulled herself to her feet and grabbed her phone. She pulled up Google and searched "Bee Spiritual Meaning."

Squinting against the yellow glare, she murmured the keywords out loud. "Personal power... Follow the rhythm of your heart... Listen to your truest self... your own inner wisdom."

Abigail ran back inside without a moment of hesitation, hastily shoving her clothes into her bag. She snatched her car keys, and the door slammed behind her as she bolted to the car just as the sky opened up into an Earth rattling downpour.

Out back, the divorce contract was caught in a gust and soared momentarily upward before being pelted down by the rain. Discarded.

JORDAN

"Don't give in and don't give up.
No matter what, don't break.
You're on the edge of something more,
even when your heart aches."

Jordan paused their singing, feeling a sense of foreboding as they looked out the window. It was raining now. They hoped wherever Abbi was, it wasn't near the shoreline. Hurricane Isaias had hit the Carolinas overnight and was now sweeping up the coast.

"Is this life, or is this pain? Let this wash away with rain."

Abigail

Abigail drove. The storm crashed. Terror rose to choke her. That was even before she saw the tornado form. Yellow. Green. The color of illness. Then gray. A sound like a siren rose into the air, the wind rising to a scream.

Debris flew, floated, crashed. The cyclone touched down in the town behind her. Had she escaped or was it too late?

Even the air in the car smelled off, like rusting metal and damp leaves. Earth. Decay. Death and doom and ruin. She stopped looking in the rearview. It was pointless. She could barely see the road ahead, but what she could see was her end.

Jordan

"Even when life batters us, this raging, waring storm,
   our white balloons will carry us home, and safe, and warm."

They stood and crossed to a window, pressing their fingertips against the glass. They leaned their guitar against their desk. "Be safe out there, Abs," they murmured, taking in the sight of the rain and clouds, like an airborne sea.

Abigail

Abbi saw her life in a flicker of snapshots, just like a scene in movies. Suppression in childhood. Hidden tears. A cruel brother. Things that were unclear and raw. Mom trying to protect her. Dad yelling. Going to food for comfort. Swallowing. Swallowing it all down. Trying to date boys.

Being teased for her weight. College. Freedom. Getting her first teaching job. The students. Her poetry.

Jory laughing.

Jory playing the guitar.

Jory proposing at the beach.

So if I should live another day, don't let it be without you. The brightest light I've ever seen, you've given me a clear view; let it be, oh let it be, that you feel the same as I do.

"I do, Jory! I do!" she cried.

She felt weightless as the car hydroplaned forward toward an unknown destination, the car propelling effortlessly and automatically, just like Jory's love for her.

TESTING

During this stage of grief, feelings of depression or hopelessness may continue; however, there will be signs of hope returning as one attempts to deal with the situation.

JORDAN

When Abbi collided directly with them, drenched, shaking, and sobbing, all Jordan could do was breathe. Anything else felt too complicated. They'd barely had time to register the door opening before Abbi was on top of them. It was as though Abbi had come back to them, not just with a crack in the dam, but like the whole dam wall had been beamed out by aliens. They'd never seen Abbi so vulnerable or broken down.

She was snotty, paler than usual, and looked like she'd been tossed in the hurricane head first.

After an onslaught of tears filled the wordless space for long enough, Abbi coughed. "I'm sorry, Jory. I'm so, so sorry."

"Where were you?" Jordan asked, dazed.

"New Jersey. Cape May."

"Oh my God, the storm hit there didn't it?"

"Yeah, right about the same time as it hit me that I'm the world's jerkiest jerk and that my family is terrible and Mom goes along with it." She sucked in a breath. "And I was going along with it too because I just always wanted her to be proud of her daughter because she has a shitty life with Dad and doesn't seem to realize women can speak up for themselves... And... And..."

"Well," Jordan said, a note of amusement creeping into their voice, "I'm glad you've come to terms with that."

"I almost died," Abbi whispered, her voice dry leaves.

"Enough death, thanks."

They felt a surge of worry as they joked, but Abbi laughed. They released a held breath and rubbed her back lovingly.

"Seriously. I almost died in other ways, too, I think. Aside from the car hydroplaning nearly into another car head-on in the middle of a hurricane and a tornado. I mean, that I almost lost myself. Lost my love for you. Lost what makes me me."

Jordan felt their throat tighten at the image of Abbi colliding head first with another car.

"Why did you drive in all that?"

"I needed to get back to you, now. And I'm here now. That's what matters, right?"

Jordan swallowed hard. Yeah. Yeah, that's what mattered.

"Yeah, Babbi..."

"I haven't been an ally. Every moment I consider excusing my mother and father's behavior and thoughts, I'm essentially saying, 'Our familial bond is stronger than my respect for the lives and feelings of women, and queer, and Black people everywhere.' And, my actions also say, 'My mom's approval is more important than the feelings of my spouse, the person I took a vow to love and protect.' I chose you back on the beach, but then my actions haven't reflected that. And they need to. I promise moving forward that I'm going to love you and honor you in truth, and not let my parent's brainwashing get in the way of that."

Jordan let the words settle down around their shoulders like a mantle of pride, hope, and love. They did know Abbi's true self after all.

"Hey. I want to show you something," they said, planting a kiss on the top of her head. "I know, topic change and all, but... Well, you'll see."

Abbi followed Jordan over to where they'd left their guitar. They picked it up, feeling the strings with their fingers and playing a few chords.

"I wrote a song while you were gone. Well, most of it. Part of it will sound familiar. I call it 'White Balloons,' but I want to know what you think."

The instrument vibrated beneath their fingers as they began to play, meeting Abbi's eyes as they sang. Each word was sung clearly, heavy with emotion. All their love. All their pain. It sounded with each syllable and note, clear as a perfect spring day.

Abbi's hands flew to her face, palms covering her eyes as she began crying once again.

It was well after midnight when Jordan and Abigail finally began dozing, their naked limbs intertwined like milky moonlight and bronze. It was as it always should have been, line upon line, circle upon circle. The air smelled like sweat, tears, and passion. It was their signature scent, the one that punctuated many long nights of lovemaking. It was the scent of oneness. Of shared experience. Of home.

The next morning they stood on the back patio, Abbi with tea, Jordan with coffee.

It took Jordan a moment to find their voice, that residual worry of somehow saying the wrong thing creeping down their neck. "You know, we already work with children so much."

"You're right," Abbi replied.

"Do you think you want to have kids, now? Be honest with me, Abs."

"No. I don't. I recognize it all now. Sure, I can't imagine being a parent with anyone but you. You'd make the world's best Renny, and I'd make a pretty good Mom. But, I think I just wanted to fill a gap that existed in my life. I thought that gap was a child, but now I see that gap was really just me not allowing myself to be me. It was the void created by all the expectations of Mom and Dad, society, the patriarchy. God. I feel... I feel almost guilty for being okay with how things are turning out now. Like... I am not happy Joscelin died at all. And yet, I wonder if she was just a messenger almost. Telling me it is okay to not go down that path. People will think I'm selfish for not having kids," Abbi said.

In unison, they finished the statement. "But that doesn't matter."

Abbi grinned at Jordan before continuing. "I don't have to have kids to be valid. There are so many things we can do with our lives that help the world around us. And honestly, like I said a while back, this pandemic is a lot. If other people want to bring children into this world, that's fine. We'll help the ones they do."

"Not to mention, we can change our mind down the road if it's really important, but only for the right reasons, kay?" Jordan said.

"Of course. But... After this, I don't think that's likely. Tell me, Jory, what do you want?"

Jordan paused to think. "I want you. I want sunshine and decoration and seeing the world. Hot cocoa and laughter. All these things can happen with kids, sure. But, they can also happen with a chosen family. With the ones we love."

"Speaking of family..." Abbi put down her tea cup on the patio table, looking out at the horizon with an expression of resolution. "I have an important call I need to make. It's time to face things head on."

Jordan watched on in awe as Abbi retrieved her phone, sat down, crossed one thick leg over the other, and called her mother.

Margie answered, and Jordan felt gooseflesh flare across their arms. That woman was unbearable to them. Her loud, abrasive voice didn't even require speakerphone to be clearly heard.

"Hello, Abigail. Did you decide to apologize for our last conversation?"

"No."

Abbi delivered the word in such a flat snap of a syllable that Jordan actually smirked.

"In fact, I wanted to see if you wanted to apologize."

"For what?" Margie said, sounding absolutely appalled at the suggestion.

"Let's see... For the time you went along with rejecting me at the holidays because of my sexual orientation. For the times you've made uneducated, racist comments. For the times you tried to force your religious views on me, your politics, and your pride. For all the times you tried to convince me to leave my loving, supportive spouse and pursue someone else, specifically a White man, while you stay married to a man that tears people down for fun."

"I never..."

"Nope. Unless you're apologizing, I don't want to hear anything else right now. I've stayed silent long enough. So continuing... For the times you continued to imply I should have children, even when I was going through all that grief over losing my child. For insisting on me trying again."

"But you always wanted them..."

"No. I always wanted to help them, that much is true. And I already do that. You were the one who always wanted grandchildren."

"But..."

"Look Mom. I know this is hard for you to hear." Abbi put her hand out for Jordan to take. "You've only ever gotten pushback from Dad and Jack, and you'd never expect your darling baby girl Abigail to hop on that bandwagon. Dad and Jack are both homophobic, racist, patriarchy loving White men. They're unlikely to ever back down from that stance. I have higher hopes for you, Mom. I know there is goodness in your heart. I know you tried as well as you could to show me I could be a strong woman and end up better off than you did. I know you go along with everything Dad says because he is terrifying and dominating. I get it.

"I will gladly talk to you again under the following conditions. One, you do not try to convince me to have children ever again. Two, you never imply I should leave Jory again. Three, you get yourself some education on white humility, racism, and what the Black Lives Matter movement is all about."

"But..."

"Until then, please leave me alone unless it's to ask for a resource. I love you, but love does not mean I have to put up with shit. Goodbye."

When she hung up the phone, Jordan couldn't possibly feel more proud of her. They kissed her tears as she folded into herself in sobs, holding her tightly. They'd never let go.

"You did good, Babbi. Real good."

Jordan explained how they'd discovered online that white balloons could symbolize grief, thus inspiring the title of their song. The couple talked about the idea of releasing their own white balloons into the sky, but Abbi was vehement that balloons caused unnecessary pollution, even if they claimed to be biodegradable. Helium was a finite resource. Their original plan had involved writing a note to Joscelin and then putting it inside or on the balloon to release it once it had been blown up. Instead, they got watercolor canvases and rented a cabin in West Virginia to complete a different sort of rite.

Abbi painted the two canvases with the outline of a white balloon, giving the sense of a background in pale blue. Each of them wrote messages in the shape, taking their time with the experience and certainly shedding many tears along the way.

When they both finished, Jordan built a campfire log by log, taking care to make it as nice a ritual as possible. This was to honor their child, after all.

"Do you want to read your message first?" Jordan asked.

"Will you go first? I'm still new to this whole sharing deep feelings thing."

"You're doing great, though," Jordan assured her.

And she was. Ever since she'd started therapy after coming home from New Jersey, now over two months ago, she had been making little steps toward sharing her feelings. She'd already overcome the worst hurdle that was challenging her mother.

Jordan lifted their canvas and began to read.

"To Joscelin -- I'm sad you're not going to tackle the patriarchy, but I guess that's a lot of pressure to put on a kid. But, you inspire me every day to really dig into the work I do with children. Every life is precious, and the ones cut short before they even begin are no exception.

"I'm glad that you got through to your Momma that day. I'm glad she came back to me. You helped us put our relationship through the ultimate test, and helped her break free from a prison she didn't know she was in. That is a lifetime's worth of work, and you managed to pack it into just a few months with your presence... And lack thereof."

Jordan paused to wipe at an eye, then glanced at Abbi. She was silently crying, watching the embers drift off the firepit and float into the air like fireflies blinking in and out.

They continued. "For all the experiences you'll never get to know in this lifetime, I hope in your next you get to experience them all, but in a brighter future than the one that exists now. I hope you live in a place where no one is judged for who they love or something as simple as the color of their skin.

"I hope you're a completely free spirit, unburdened by judgment, hatred, or limitation. You're our little bumble bee, and you'll never be otherwise. May you visit us every year and remind us what it means to love. Love, Renny."

Jordan watched Abbi struggle to suck down a breath, dab at her eyes with her fleece poncho, and pick up her own canvas. They offered a reassuring smile at her.

Abbi cleared her throat delicately. "Dear Joscelin... I'll never know what you could have been, but I do know what you were. A whisper. A reminder. A call to adventure. You were the mentor, the threshold, and the test all in one, but you were not the ordeal, nor the battle I won. Every bumble bee that buzzes, every tear I cry, I'll remember how I loved you, and how no one ever truly says goodbye. I'll feel you in the springtime, in the summer, and the rain. I'll feel you in the good times, and all my times of pain. No matter what I go through, no matter where I've been, I'll hold on to my truest self, and see you once again."

A laugh cracked her composure a moment. "I'm lousy with rhyming poems, aren't I?" she said, looking over at Jordan.

"Nah. It was sweet." They meant it, rubbing at the hem of their hoodie.

Abbi looked back at her canvas. "Maybe this whole thing did break me, but in the end... I found my actual self underneath all the rubble. So, thank you Joscelin." With that, she stood, and moved toward the fire.

"Shall we?"

Jordan crossed to stand next to her, wrapping an arm around her. The flames licked up toward the twilight sky, flickering like their hope had along the way. As they both leaned in and gingerly placed their canvases, the fire consumed them with a brilliant blaze of light, and before they could even register as burning, they were gone. Much like Joscelin's brief life.

"I love you, Jory," Abbi whispered, leaning into them.

"I love you, too, Babbi. And Josie. Always."

ACCEPTANCE

Acceptance may feel a long way off, but everyone gets there in the end. Pain may still exist, but it no longer feels insufferable. Able to make plans for the future and enjoy living again, it is the final stage of grief.

Abigail

Jor approached with a steaming mug of cocoa, sitting down beside Abigail in front of the digital fireplace. They enjoyed their drinks for a long while, sitting in silence. Peace. Hope. Love. Life had gotten complicated for a while, but that was okay. They'd made it through.

"What do we do if this pandemic keeps going indefinitely, or it gets better and then worse?" Abigail asked, cupping her empty mug.

"We learn new skills together. We cook a lot. We have extra sex?"

"Weren't we doing all of that more or less already?"

"Yeah," Jor said, shrugging. "But, it is what it is."

"You've got that right. And, honestly, I'm okay with that."

Abigail looked over at Jory fondly, rubbing a hand against the side of their head. Their fade cut was back, and that little detail almost made it feel like everything was back to normal. Their relationship was in a sort of golden era, better than it had felt, even in the beginning. It was admittedly so peaceful without Margie nagging her incessantly over babies and racist stuff. There was a sadness in that, but also so much space.

With the cocoa done, Jor helped Abbi set up a black Christmas tree, like the one they'd seen in the window about a year ago. They strung up the golden garland together, and Abigail found herself humming. Jor smiled over at her, and her heart went off like sparklers. It was nice to not only have the energy back in their relationship but to just be thriving in general. Abigail had figured out how to gamify her classroom and was surprisingly enjoying online teaching. Of course, it was winter break for now, but she was actually looking forward to going back in January. She prayed to whoever would listen that 2021 was better than 2020, though, and that the world would achieve a new normal like she and Jory had.

Just as they were stringing lights on the tree, there came a knock at the door.

Jordan bound over and opened it. Erica and Alex were standing there, Alex holding a large box tightly. Erica had a pretty fancy-looking mask on with an air filter and eye protection.

"You know, I admire your dedication to health," Jor said, "But we did get tested right before I went on vacation."

As they were ushered in, Alex walked toward the kitchen with the box. Jordan shut the door with a clap behind them.

"Fair... But, don't mind me if I still don't hug you," Erica said, grinning as she took her mask off.

"What's in the box?" Abigail asked, taking a step toward the group.

"A surprise I planned for you," Jor said. "With their help."

"Now, now. Wait for the big reveal and the story," Erica said. "There has been a lot of loss this year. A lot of grief. But, sometimes after loss comes an incredible opportunity. So, I present to you..."

Erica paused dramatically waiting for Alex to do something. When he didn't, she walked over and prodded him in the side.

"Ah!" He sat the box down and opened the flaps.

There was nothing, then a cat leapt out from within.

"That's Oscar," Erica said, indicating the pure white feline.

Abigail felt like she might implode with joy. Oscar was a chubby little guy, and quite curious. He stalked with singular focus over to her and batted playfully at her skirt. "Awww..."

"This in here is Poppy... She's a mackerel tabby."

Abigail moved so she could see down into the box. There was a petite tabby cat nestled into the towel at the bottom. She looked to be rather timid.

"Poppy is shy," Erica affirmed.

"Well, I don't know about their names," Jor said. "We'll go with that for now, but you know, if their true colors shine through later, we can always rename them. I'm quite keen on embracing the name that's right for you when the time comes."

"Yeah you are." Abigail gave Jor's bottom a playful slap, then knelt to try and comfort Poppy. "Hi baaaaby," she cooed.

Poppy lifted her head.

"She kind of looks like a bumble bee with those stripes," Abigail realized with a slight start.

"They're a bonded pair," Erica said. "Their owners, unfortunately, passed on from COVID and they were brought into the shelter recently. Now you can be their parents."

Abigail sniffed and Jory put a hand on her shoulder.

"See, Babbi, we can still be parents without kids. Isn't that the best?"

"It is." Already, she was beyond fond of Poppy's sweetness.

The four of them wound up laying on the floor in the living room looking up at the icicle lights around the ceiling. Alex fell asleep, snoring, and Erica just shook her head at him. The cats tentatively prowled around, checking the house out. Poppy twitched with every out-of-place sound, and Abbi felt for her. She'd been through a lot losing her prior owners. It was okay to be startled.

When there was another knock at the door, Abigail answered it. This time it was Josh with a bottle of wine and a cake in tow.

"What kinda cake is it?" Alex asked, sitting up and suddenly awake.

"Fruit."

Alex groaned.

"Josh!" Jor said. "Congratulations. You're an Uncle!"

Before he could question it, Oscar was there, taking a bat at Josh's shoelaces.

"Oh shit!" He crouched down and gave Oscar a scratch behind the ears. "Hey lil' bud."

Abigail smiled until her face hurt.

After enjoying some wonderful takeout from *foraged.*, the five friends decorated the tree with a variety of gold, black, and yellow ornaments. When all of them had been placed, Abigail got down the box she'd been saving as a surprise.

"I thought this ornament would be fitting for this year." She handed it to Jory.

Jor opened the box slowly and peered down inside.

It was a bumble bee ornament, different from the one they'd seen in the window on 34th Street. It was more refined, regal in a way.

"It's really beautiful, Abbi," Jor said.

Abigail smirked. "Just like our love.

"You two are so gay." Josh shook his head, rolling his eyes before winking at Alex.

"We are," Jor and Abigail said together.

Everyone laughed, and Abigail didn't know if she could be any happier than she was in this breath—until she watched Oscar take a swipe at the Christmas tree and get booped in the snoot by an ornament in retaliation. Now she couldn't be any happier than she was.

After everyone went home, Abigail and Jory snuggled in on the couch, dozing with the heat from the fireplace. The last year seemed like ten, even though for most of it she'd been asleep either literally or metaphorically. Her growth, and Jory's, were tremendous. She was opening up more than ever now, and Jory was speaking up for themself rather than giving in to her every whim. They actually challenged her when she had a genuinely silly idea or one that would require more planning. Something Abigail had learned about herself along the way was that she did like a good plan, but she often over-planned where she really didn't need to, and under-planned when she ought to be taking it slow. Most importantly, she'd learned that it was acceptable to dream, but her dreams were her own, not something someone else could determine for her.

Sleepily, Abigail said, "Maybe I'll write a book soon, after all."

"Oh?"

"Yeah, I might call it Bumble Bees and White Balloons. It has a nice ring to it, don't you think? Alliteration is always prime."

"It does sound nice, but what would it be about?"

"I'm not sure. Maybe it's dystopian? Fantasy? Maybe it's a sad sapphic poetry book. Or, maybe it's just a slice of life."

Jordan pulled her tighter, kissing her neck. "You're my slice of life."

"That... Doesn't even remotely make sense, but I'll take it."

"It's just weird Jory language for—"

"I love you," they said in unison, giggled, and then bumped faces as they both swooped in for a kiss.

December 25th, 2020

Bumble Bees and White Balloons

On your little bumbly wings, do you carry
all my dreams? Or are they instead
on white balloons, tangled in their strings?
What happens to a dream deferred?
I know this one sure exploded.
Ember sparks and bursts of flame,
the brightest stars imploded.
Blink, flicker, flash.

Buzz, Buzz,
bursting, surging free —
Take to the air and soar beyond,
Beyond
into my sacred sleep.
Visit me in the silent spaces
where no dream goes forgotten,
and with each breath, I'll smile peace,
rememb'ring all you taught us.
Although this life cannot contain you, each moment of joy I live and
word I speak can carry with it your memory, my bumble bee.

— Momma Abbi

Thank you for reading.

Q&A with the Author

How often do authors put themselves out there? I don't just mean their work–publishing itself is incredibly vulnerable. But, I mean putting themselves on display as the person who brought the writing into the world.

I've read many books and explored more author websites than I can count, but I often find there is little more than a general author bio. While this is standard and perfectly acceptable (we all have boundaries), I've always enjoyed knowing who the book's author is beyond the surface. Delving into their humanity. Understanding their worldview and inspiration.

What can I say? I'm a people person! I love authenticity, connection, and genuine compassion.

Writing is an exploration of the soul, a means to dive into our psyche, our schema of life, and the parts of ourselves that may otherwise never have a voice.

I know I'm not the only one who enjoys getting to know writers! So just in case you're one of those people, I added this bonus section to this work so you can understand ME, the author, a little bit more.

What inspired you to write this book? Was there a specific personal experience, news event, social issue, etc, that sparked the idea?

Bumble Bees & White Balloons was originally written in September 2020 as a part of the 3-Day Novel Contest. While this book did not win the competition, I walked away from the experience with a pretty decent manuscript and a whole lot of emotional processing completed. The year I entered the contest was 2020–the year the world was rocked by the COVID-19 crisis. No matter who you were or where you were from, you WERE impacted by that event. We all were, and I think, still are.

As I circled around to what to write for the contest, this book surfaced. In 2012, I lost my daughter Shaina to anencephaly, the same neural tube defect Abigail and Jordan's child had in this novel. I had never heard of this rare medical condition until I myself experienced my own devastating loss.

In the months after, I suffered mostly in silence. A majority of people in my life just thought I had a miscarriage and all the unpleasantness that involved. For me it was a time of deep questioning, pretty much around my entire life. Many of these same questions arise in this book, though the timelines are completely different.

Combine the experience of pregnancy loss, which isn't really talked about in a lot of books, with the feelings of isolation brought about by COVID. It makes it more relatable, I think, to have it layered in with something that everyone can understand. So when I was choosing the setting and time period for this book, I knew originally that I was working on something related to my own experiences of pregnancy loss, but the pandemic gave it a far more emotional backdrop even than the original event itself.

For me as a person with medical trauma, I don't need the pandemic to respond to the trauma of the story. However, everyone can relate to how much fear there was at the time of the pandemic. So juxtaposing these two emotionally intense situations just heightens that sense of trauma and the challenges to overcome that. I myself have experienced, as have many people who have experienced pregnancy loss, that sense of being isolated and misunderstood. Setting this in the pandemic added an extra layer as the extra isolation and the medical fear is heightened in this setting.

What were your initial goals in writing this book? How did you hope it would impact your readers?

My initial goal in writing this book was to prove to myself that I could write a book in three days! I tend to do my best writing when there is some kind of deadline and an audience.

Because I was entering a contest, I knew people would be reading this. I wanted the novel to be something emotionally profound, poetic, and beautiful that would move readers. I know it made a lasting impression on my alpha and beta readers!

Ultimately, however, I want everyone that reads it to be able to take away hope, even in the face of the darkest of times because the book does not pull punches on the hard stuff.

In this book, I explore the pandemic, racism, body image issues, and queer issues–all topics that aren't to be taken lightly. But these are also all topics that aren't really explored often in fiction that I've seen. I'm sure they exist, but I haven't read many. I want this book to get in people's faces in a way–to encourage them to understand their impact, the impact of global events, and the impact of certain circumstances that might arise in people's lives that they may never understand.

For example, Abigail and me as a White person can't fully understand Jordan's experience as a Black person, but through the book, people might be able to get a glimpse into what it might be like to experience these challenges.

What might happen if we were open minded about each other's experiences?

Over the writing process, did the book end up going in a different direction than you originally planned?

Honestly, there wasn't anything planned about this book. Since I sat down to write this book in three days, I didn't have an outline until the day before, and I just made the decision to explore the relationship between these two characters in the vague circumstances I'd decided to set them.

However, in the rewriting process, I was surprised by the Erica chapter. When I had originally written the manuscript, it was around 35,000 words in the first draft, and I decided since I didn't win the contest to extend it to a more "full length romance novel," which is about 50,000 words. So I added in some content with Josh and Erica, that I didn't ever intend on being there. It was not in the first draft at all, so the presence of that surprised me.

There was a time in which all of the representations of queer characters were like them suffering or being killed, bullied, ostracized, etc for being queer. There was no happy ending and queer stories. While the concept of pregnancy loss was at the forefront, I knew the characters would stay together in the end because I didn't want it to be just another really, really sad lesbian story. I knew I wanted there to be a happy ending, but didn't really know what form that would take.

I am pretty pleased with it being cats in the end. I really love cats. ;)

Discuss any research you did and relate it to the themes of the book. How did you strive for accurate representation?

I did so much research for this book. All of the medical things that were experienced were things I experienced, so it's as accurate as it can be from somebody who was traumatized in the midst of the experience itself (just to account for the dubiousness in memory). However, I did a ton of research about the timeline of things because it's actually set in the real world.

The School District, for example–I actually looked into when the schools closed down. How did they announce it?

What were medical offices doing in terms of pregnancies and going in to get procedures done and all of that. I really tried to look into what the norms were in those regions at that time and how real businesses were being impacted by the pandemic. As mentioned in the author's note at the beginning, I did reach out to the owner of *foraged.* and Atomic Books because they were places I myself frequented pre-pandemic.

There was quite a bit of historical research and diversity research. I worked with two Black sensitivity readers for Jordan to ensure I was respectfully and appropriately exploring the African American and Black perspective from Jordan's POV.

Of course Jordan is a fictional character, but they're not just a fictional character in a fantasy world where the color of their skin may or may not play a role in the politics of the world. This book is very much set in our real world of 2020, and I wanted to ensure that Jordan was being depicted and written in such a way that explored the real kinds of feelings that one might have as a Person of Color during that time.

No two people are the same and there is no way to account for each and every person's feelings on this planet. I hope, however, to have written a piece with relatable characters showcasing a wide range of experiences.

Name some of your favorite authors or books that influenced your writing. How do they shape your style in the book?

Maya Angelou is definitely my role model, personally, and as a poet and an autobiographical writer–just a prolific writer in general. She was somebody who spoke through symbolism on issues of injustice in the world. She was Black, experienced atrocities, and still stood as a fierce advocate for others who were marginalized, such as the LGBTQIA+ community. Her writing is incredible, so poetic, yet straightforward.

I Know Why the Caged Bird Sings, her autobiography, and *Caged Bird*, a poem, are two of the pieces that have most influenced me.

She talks about child abuse, sexual trauma, and all of all of this really awful stuff that happened to her; yet threaded through her work are themes of hope and triumph. As a Black woman, she overcame so much to get her voice out there. She was incredibly successful in her self-expression. She received the National Medal of Arts amongst numerous other awards and honorary degrees. Maya Angelou has always been an inspiration to me about not staying silent, even though I've endured atrocities.

What do you hope readers will take away from this book? What feelings or realizations do you hope to evoke?

I cried while reading this book back!

I hope that it elicits some intense emotion in readers because I think that's the sign of a good piece of writing, but I don't hope to make people overwhelmingly sad. I just want them to understand the impact that these circumstances have on people because there's so little discussion in society about our feelings.

It's very rare for us to deep dive into how trauma makes us feel. How isolation makes us feel. How other people's actions and interactions make us feel.

It is my dream that this book will lead to some needed conversations and healing.

I hope that if anyone else is struggling with racism in their family, or homophobia, transphobia, lack of boundaries, or anything else explored here, that a book like this might make them realize that those things are harmful.

Even if something doesn't affect us directly, how we react or don't react to certain circumstances ends up impacting other people. That's literally part of my big role here on Earth: to help people understand the impact that we have on one another as living beings, as well as the planet herself.

What has been the most rewarding part of writing this book? What have you learned during the process?

The most rewarding part of writing this book was writing it and getting it done! This is not the first book I've ever written, but it's the first book I'm ever going to publish. To have it be such a vulnerable piece that I'm publishing first is a big deal.

I'm not hiding behind my alias for my sci fi adventures or even a pen name. This book is me. It's my style. It's my voice. It is my essence in a book.

To have had people read it and tell me that it emotionally impacted them has been very rewarding. It made them think. It made them laugh. All of those things are the rewards.

By stepping more into visibility and bringing this book to anyone who wants to read it, my work has the capacity to directly encourage people I have never met to think, feel, and maybe even create! That is the biggest reward!

What would you want readers to know about the personal importance of this story and why you felt compelled to tell them?

I think that writing is one of the most powerful ways that we can process things.

In the future, I'll be offering workshops on how to draw on parts of ourselves to create characters. That was a lot of what this book was about: drawing on parts of myself to feed them into the characters, making them both very real as well as reprocessing things I needed to look at from a different angle.

Until writing this book I had never addressed the loss of my daughter. I used all kinds of other methods to avoid looking at it or make it okay. This book fully allowed me to make it okay because not only is it honoring my daughter, but it is honoring other people who have experienced similar.

In a far different way, this book is still birthing something. It's still a legacy of that experience that I get to leave behind. So I needed to write this book for me first, and now it gets to be for everyone else.

How do you think this book could promote empathy, spark dialogue, and bring about positive change in society?

I understand that if certain people pick up this book, it's going to make them very angry. This book works with stereotypes and the reality that presently there are groups of people who are divided.

There's a lot of division in this book: political division, racial division, division caused by harmful opinions around bodies, sexuality, and gender.

I hope that by being so direct and upfront about the harm of these things and exploring the impact, empathy can be created. It's possible to empathize with both main characters, but I really hope that more than anything people empathize with Jordan.

Jordan represents the silenced people. Abigail does too with aspects of her own identity, but Jordan represents people with a lack of privilege whose voices may never be heard. I hope that people who feel like their voices are not being heard will take encouragement from Jordan, coming into their own in the end and deciding to speak up. It can be scary (and even dangerous) to live authentically in this world, but I think it's the most important thing we can do.

I really hope that there's a character everyone can relate to in some way. By calling out family dynamics or phobias that people have, I hope we can start to unpack them and have open conversations in a way that frees us from having to carry these burdens around all the time.

These are uncomfortable feelings to explore and topics to discuss. Yet, it's by us feeling uncomfortable that we grow. This is my concept of Shadow Alchemy: how discomfort is literally what moves us into our next layers of expansion.

So yes, I hope this book makes people uncomfortable and inspires them to be greater, more expansive, more in love with life, humanity, and the planet than they ever knew they could be.

This book is not just a journey through the shadows of society and relationships, but a beacon towards a brighter, more understanding world. As you navigate the complexities and divisions within these pages, I'm inviting you to reflect on your own perspectives and biases, to challenge the status quo and engage in meaningful, sometimes difficult conversations. It's in these brave spaces of openness and vulnerability that seeds of empathy and unity are planted.

My hope is that this book serves as a mirror and a window – a mirror reflecting our own truths, however uncomfortable they may be, and a window into the lives and struggles of those different from ourselves. It is through understanding these diverse experiences that we forge a path to a more compassionate and inclusive society.

Let this book be a reminder that our collective humanity is enriched, not diminished, by our differences.

May it inspire you to embrace your own authenticity, to raise their voices for justice and equality, and to recognize that in the tapestry of human experience, every thread, every color, every pattern is essential.

Together, we can turn discomfort into action, division into unity, and shadows into light. It is in our collective courage to confront and transform the shadows that we find our greatest strength and our most profound capacity to love and change the world.

In Solidarity, Love, and Courage,
Safrianna Lughna

Book Club Suggestions

Creating a Trauma-Informed Book Discussion Circle

Bumble Bees and White Balloons explores sensitive topics like pregnancy loss, mental health, and racial trauma that may be triggering for some readers. Here are some tips for facilitating a thoughtful, compassionate discussion:

- Provide content warnings about potentially distressing subject matter so members can make informed decisions about participation. Discuss establishing group norms around giving these warnings.

- Don't require sharing. Allow members to participate at their own comfort level and don't pressure anyone to speak.

- If members do share personal experiences, listen with empathy and refrain from judgment or advice-giving. Validate their feelings.

- Interrupt and redirect any insensitive or harmful comments, but don't shame. Gently guide members to think critically about impact vs intent.

- Invite a diverse group and be mindful of dynamics. Consider an anti-racism trainer or mental health professional as a co-facilitator if the themes require it.

- Balance complex themes with lighter discussion and even laughter. Make space for joy and rest.

- Have a list of mental health resources on hand that members can take. Follow up with members who need additional support.

- Give trigger warnings before meeting so members can mentally and emotionally prepare. Allow members to discreetly exit if needed.

- Agree to confidentiality so members feel safe sharing vulnerable thoughts and feelings.

We can create book discussion groups with compassion and care that build understanding while preventing further harm or trauma. Consider members' well-being first when facilitating.

Below are some discussion questions that may be used by any discussion groups that want to work with this book:

Discussion Questions

1. Why do you think Abigail reacted the way she did to the trauma and grief of losing her pregnancy? Have you or someone you know experienced something similar?

2. Discuss the relationship between Abigail and her mother. In what ways did her upbringing impact her choices as an adult?

3. How did external events like the pandemic and racial injustice highlight cracks in Abigail and Jordan's relationship? Have global events ever affected your personal relationships?

4. When have you realized something new or unexpected about yourself, like Abigail did on her journey? How did that change your perspective?

5. Jordan mentions feeling like an "imposter" in their grief over the baby. Why do you think they felt this way? Have you ever experienced grief over something others didn't think you had a right to grieve?

6. How did each character change and grow over the course of the story? What do you think they learned? How have pivotal moments in your life led to personal growth or change? What were some of the biggest lessons?

7. Discuss the symbolism of the bumble bee and the white balloons. What did they come to represent? What objects or symbols take on deeper meaning in your own life, like the bumble bee and white balloons did for Abigail and Jordan?

8. What did you find most relatable about this story? What resonated with you personally?

9. Think about a relationship you have that has been tested similarly to Abigail and Jordan. How did you maintain the bond? What advice would you give others based on it?

10. If you went through a similar awakening journey,

what do you think you would discover about
yourself? What would you change?

Resources

Below are links to organizations, charities, and educational resources related to some of the issues and themes explored in Bumble Bees and White Balloons. Remember that resources do exist for a variety of issues and that it is okay to seek and ask for help! You are not alone.

Pregnancy and Infant Loss Support

Share Pregnancy & Infant Loss Support: Offers support for those affected by the loss of a baby due to pregnancy loss, stillbirth, or in the early months of life. https://nationalshare.org/

Rachel's Gift: Provides support groups and collaborates with hospitals to offer care for parents experiencing miscarriage, stillbirth, or infant death.
https://www.rachelsgift.org/

LGBTQ+ Family Resources

Family Equality: Provides a virtual support space for LGBTQ+ parents of school-aged children and promotes LGBTQ+ family equality. https://www.familyequality.org/

Strong Family Alliance: Offers support and resources to parents of LGBTQ+ children, focusing on the coming out process. https://www.strongfamilyalliance.org/

PFLAG: A discussion series for LGBTQ+ and ally issues, providing ongoing support and resources. https://pflag.org/

Racial Justice and Anti-Racism Education

Center for Racial Justice in Education: Offers trainings for educators and organizations to understand and disrupt systems perpetuating racism. https://centerracialjustice.org/

WE: Provides an anti-racism module for understanding and taking action on anti-racism in schools and communities. https://www.we.org/

NAACP: The NAACP actively works on issues such as criminal justice reform, health equity, economic opportunity, and education with a mission to ensure the equality of rights of all persons and to eliminate racial hatred and racial discrimination. https://naacp.org/

Domestic Violence/Abuse Assistance

National Domestic Violence Hotline: Provides 24/7 support for survivors of domestic violence. https://www.thehotline.org/

NCADV: Provides resources for victims and survivors of domestic violence. https://ncadv.org/

Mental Health and Grief

American Counseling Association: Offers resources for grief and loss, including articles, practice briefs, and books, as well as many other mental health related topics. https://www.counseling.org

Mental Health America: Provides insights into the

process of bereavement and grief, as well as support resources, information, and opportunities for advocacy. https://www.mhanational.org/

NAMI (National Alliance on Mental Illness): The largest grassroots mental health organization in the U.S., offering support for various mental health issues. https://www.nami.org/Home

Relationship Support Resources

The Gottman Institute: Provides relationship and marriage advice, tips, and therapy resources. https://www.gottman.com/couples/

About the Author

Safrianna Lughna, known widely as the Queer-Spirit Guide, is not only an influential author but also a Healer of Healers. Her writing deeply intertwines with her life experiences, offering rich insights and transformative narratives. As a therapist and educator, Safrianna employs her intuitive gifts to guide fellow health professionals, spiritual entrepreneurs, creatives, and visionaries through their journeys of personal and professional growth.

In her authorship, Safrianna transcends the conventional, blending creativity with intuitive healing and spiritual channeling. Her literary work is a reflection of her approach to healing, guiding readers from trauma to triumph through compelling and insightful narratives.

At the heart of her writing and healing practice is Living LUNA, a sanctuary she founded for authenticity and self-empowerment. This platform is a gathering space for those who resonate with being "weird" and "woo," promoting upliftment and personal growth. Safrianna's focus extends to individuals grappling with the nuances of queer and polyamorous identities, as well as business owners managing unseen chronic conditions.

A passionate advocate for LGBTQIA+ and polyamorous rights, Safrianna's voice reaches thousands through her writing, podcasts, courses, and rituals.

She is an international best-selling author whose writings are a beacon for those she affectionately calls the "Others," providing guidance and inspiration to live beyond societal conventions.

In her personal time, Safrianna writes poetry and science fiction, plays thought-provoking video games, and cherishes moments with her chosen family, including many cats.

Discover more about Safrianna's unique journey and works at https://Safrianna.com cr https://LivingLUNAs.com. She welcomes connections and inquiries at Coach@Safrianna.com.